# Twenty-Five Sanitary Inspectors

Superintendent Simmonds had recently retired from the CID. The last thing he wanted was to find himself again in charge of a murder case. But strange events in the tiny, delectable West Indian island republic of San Rocco proved too strong for him. When the Acropolis Theatre, Cinema and Hotel in that 'Athens of the West Indies' suffered murder, fire and sabotage in short order, Simmonds had no option but to become involved. How he must have sighed for the days when he had a force of trained and experienced detectives at his command. For San Rocco had a distinct shortage of detectives, and to repair this lack a force of twenty-five sanitary inspectors was hastily recruited to assist him in investigating the mystery. Nevertheless, this entertaining and civilized novel rapidly generates enough excitement to satisfy even the most demanding reader.

This title was first published in the Crime Club in 1935.

ROGER EAST

# Twenty-Five Sanitary Inspectors

Superintendent Simmonds investigates . . .

## The Disappearing Detectives
*Selected and Introduced*
*by H. R. F. Keating*

COLLINS, 8 GRAFTON STREET, LONDON W1

William Collins Sons & Co. Ltd
London · Glasgow · Sydney · Auckland
Toronto · Johannesburg

First published in the Crime Club 1935
Reprinted in this edition 1985
Copyright reserved Roger East
© in the Introduction, H. R. F. Keating, 1985

British Library Cataloguing in Publication Data

East, Roger
Twenty-five sanitary inspectors.—
(The Disappearing detectives)
—(Crime Club)
I. Title    II. Series
823′.912[F]        PR6009.A7/

ISBN 0 00 231995 0

Photoset in Linotron Baskerville by
Rowland Phototypesetting Ltd
Bury St Edmunds, Suffolk
Printed in Great Britain by
William Collins Sons & Co. Ltd, Glasgow

For
V.L.E.

# INTRODUCTION
## H. R. F. Keating

It is a salutary thought for a writer of crime fiction today
that a fellow practitioner who on the appearance of his first
book *Murder Rehearsal* in 1933 evoked from the *Manchester
Evening Chronicle*'s 'Dr Watson' the question 'Who in the
world is Mr Roger East?' with the addition: 'It is my
considered opinion that he seems likely to become one of
the small band of really first-class detective story writers,'
and whose subsequent books produced confirmatory critical
comments like 'one of the best-written detective stories I
have read for a long time' and 'a flavour of exquisite intelligence' should have disappeared almost from human ken.
But I have been unable to find the name Roger East in any
of the who's-whos and encyclopaedias of crime fiction and
his books proved almost untraceable save in the depths of
the British Library or in the files (devilish dusty, to tell the
truth) of Collins Crime Club.

But such has been the fate both of Mr East and of his
detective, Superintendent 'Simmy' Simmonds. It is a fate
from which even a book with as intriguing a title as *Twenty-
five Sanitary Inspectors* was unable to save him. But it was an
undeserved fate. Superintendent Simmonds is not only an
interesting and sympathetic character in his own right, but
he was also something of a phenomenon in crime fiction.
Perhaps in this he was before his time and that may account,
together with the fact that his creator retired him at the
start of this his fourth appearance, for his all but total
vanishing.

Superintendent Simmonds manifesting himself in *Murder
Rehearsal* entered the criminous stage unobtrusively, as befit-
ted a solid investigator, with a mild rebuke to a Chief
Constable who in the traditional way of detective fiction

7

had 'called in the Yard'. 'I don't suppose,' he said, 'you'd have brought me down to investigate a suicide.' That and no more. Yet brief though the remark is, it gives us the flavour of the man. He is independent, inclined to be caustic and has no very high opinion of most of his fellow mortals. He was, too, be it said, seen as one of the top police detectives of his day.

Heavily fat with a face that in repose 'bore the likeness to a sly Buddha', he often defied the common image of the stout man as jolly by being reserved, bitter and pessimistic, though he can rise to jovial joshing if that is the best way to get something out of a witness. 'Only a few,' wrote his creator, 'knew of his real charm, of the integrity of his mind and of his charitableness.' Already we see a protrait of a complex human being, rather than a mere set of striking characteristics, and during the Superintendent's subsequent exploits the portrait is made to seem to live.

We have had a hint that he is a true policeman as opposed to a more or less interesting person popped into police uniform (or mufti) for the convenience of an author needing a decent succession of confrontations with corpses. And it is Superintendent Simmonds's policemanliness that is the difference between him and the fictional detectives of his day. There were, of course, others who set about their cases in much the way real policemen did. I am thinking in particular of Freeman Wills Crofts's Inspector French, another stalwart of the Crime Club. But French, for all his appearance of sticking to police routine, was not in fact so much a police investigator as an *alter ego* for his methodical ex-engineer creator (and he was capable of flouting proper police methods, as Crofts would charmingly admit).

No, Superintendent Simmonds, though encased more or less in the traditional format of the detective story, was in a fair way to being a hero of the 'police procedural', a type of book which did not in fact come into being in this country until the mid-1950s with John Creasey's Commander Gideon novels (or possibly in the 1940s with some of the books of Henry Wade, son of a Metropolitan Magistrate). But in *Murder Rehearsed* Simmy Simmonds is seen regarding crime in a decidedly professional way as 'a manifestation which could be classified and punished with the impersonality of an expert, rather than with any formal fervour'. There are, too, numerous instances in each of the books of him applying strictly police methods to the cases in front of him, even in this affair where he is in the least police-like of arenas. 'Detection, he knew, is hard work and nothing else,' his creator writes of him amid the steamy tropical atmosphere of San Rocco, that invented West Indies isle.

San Rocco, indeed, is one of the pleasures of this book, surely a creation which only a poet owing allegiance, however tenuous, to Coleridge's Xanadu could have brought into being, a delightful *jeu d'esprit*. But there are realities in San Rocco, too. They add a counter-note to the fantasy, which paradoxically helps to make it seem more true. And, since the book was published in 1935, one or two of its realities of social observation may jar today (which, of course, makes them all the more interesting). Contemporary readers will not baulk morally at 'Vim', once the universal cleaning powder, and perhaps they will rejoice over the days when a car that could touch 60 m.p.h. was considered really something. But at the singling out of 'Jews' in a list of the denizens of San Rocco's marvellous dance floor they may blench a little and they may sigh at Britain seen without tongue in cheek as 'the nation famed for the honourableness of its dealings'. Yet such things once were, and it is no bad thing to have a record of them.

Of Roger East, their recorder, who disappeared from the crime writing scene almost as wholly as Simmy Simmonds, I have been able to learn a little. His real name was Roger d'Este Burford and he was indeed a poet. He died in 1981, having written in the 1950s and 60s three more crime novels after ceasing with the coming of World War II to chronicle Superintendent Simmonds's cases. During the war he worked in our embassy in Moscow and thereafter his talents were devoted chiefly to film and television scriptwriting (some of the Maigret series were from his pen). He published an autobiographical work, *Moscow Blues*, in 1974. The rest is silence.

# CHAPTER 1

## TROUBLE IN ROCCO

Calcagno was standing in the foyer of the Acropolis Theatre of San Rocco. A few patrons, millionaires mostly, late or bored, mounted or descended the marble stairs proving, each one, the high-class silence of the white and liver-coloured carpet, which had been woven to order and at enormous expense to match the marble balustrades and the fountain which spurted up through the open roof towards the glittering stars.

'Good evening, Calcagno.'

'Good evening, Señor Calcagno.'

'Better late than never, what? Calcagno?'

'Well, how are things, you old son of a bitch?'

To which Calcagno, manager of the Acropolis Theatre, replied:

'Good evening, sir and madam; good evening excellency; good evening my lord; very well, thank you, Mr Curtis.'

In the auditorium the famous rolling roof was open to the sky, and through the gigantic opening streamed the smoke of cigars, waste perfumes, the whisper of a lover, the snores of His Excellency the President, and the exhausted breath of a troupe of dancers who were stepping out one more encore than had been demanded. They alone wore clothing suited to the sultry atmosphere, but sweat was pouring down between their shoulder-blades and the powder had vanished from their arms and calves.

In the principal box his Excellency Don Miguel de Valuque, President of the Republic of San Rocco, was fast asleep, but, even though his thin sensitive lip trembled with expirations it would be ungenerous to call snores, he still looked presidential and distinguished. The fifty American dancing girls were no novelty for Don Miguel: every night for a week there had been an official banquet, and each set of official guests had desired entertainment: and that, in San Rocco, meant a visit to the Acropolis Theatre, or the Acropolis Cinema, or the Acropolis Hotel. The cinema, this week, had been showing a film from Russia, extremely worthy and depressingly tendentious. The hotel, with its dance floor and cabaret, was still suspect. A rumour that there had been several cases of yellow fever among the hotel staff had been strenuously refuted, but the wife of his Excellency considered it unnecessary for him to expose himself to even a rumour. So Don Miguel slept, the vice-President-elect let out his corsets a little, the girls pranced, the orchestra plucked and blew, and Calcagno studied his watch for the hundredth time.

The Carnation was late: half an hour late at the very least: her act was immediately after the American girls, and before the first interval. The girls had been ordered to make the most of their encores, and the telephone had buzzed between the theatre and the Carnation's villa. It was reported there that she had left at her usual time and promptly. The dresser who usually accompanied her had arrived at the theatre much earlier, having been sent on before to make some purchases in the town for her mistress. It was she who had brought the disturbing news to Calcagno. And how disturbing! All these millionaires had not come to see the American dancing girls, nor the acrobats, nor to hear the tenor. They had paid, and paid luxury prices, to see the Carnation, sensation and speciality of San Rocco. All the others they could see anywhere, but to see the Carnation they must come in their yachts or in cruising steamers from New York, Los Angeles via Panama, New Orleans, Rio de Janeiro, Buenos Aires, or even from Europe. Pero Zaragoza, genius creator and sole controller of the group of buildings which bore the name of the Acropolis, aimed only at one clientèle—that of the richest men in the world. That mountain of white marble, towering on a rocky hill above the capital town of 'the Athens of the West Indies', could only be supported by the patronage of the most wealthy: for them

12

the dance floor that floated unnecessarily on quicksilver, the iced water laid on to every cocktail cabinet in every apartment, the separate brocaded arm-chairs in the theatre, the flowers which greeted their arrival, and the basket of tropical fruit waiting for them in their state-rooms when they departed: for them the Carnation, eccentric dancer from Mexico, the supreme creation of Pero and of her own will.

Don Miguel had asked to be wakened as soon as she appeared: it was the première of a new dance in honour of the gala night, which was in honour of the birthday of the Minister of the Interior—such birthdays always conveniently coincided with the arrival of a cruising steamer or the yacht of a meat king—and if in his heart of hearts he would have preferred to be playing chess at home, a president may least of all ignore the conventions. A bouquet of flowers and bird-of-paradise feathers had been prepared for him to give her—it meant a centimo rate throughout the island.

Calcagno, alone now, gazed anxiously down the winding motor road, flood-lit and fringed with palm trees. A step on the gravel made him turn sharply, his hand travelling towards a bulging hip pocket. But it was only the stage manager, begging for advice.

'Sir, the position must be faced; if the intermission is announced, we can no longer hide the fact that the Carnation is missing. If it is not to be announced, then what am I to do? From the second half there is no number I can use as a finale. It is impossible to alter the order of events, either for one reason or another. I—'

'What is that?' Calcagno suddenly pointed down the road. Immediately below them, at the bottom of the zigzag a car had begun to mount.

'Her automobile!'

'Is it?'

'It looks like it!'

'Then don't stand here gazing—she may yet be in time. Send the girls on once more.'

'I will, I will, I will.' The stage manager sped away with

swallows at his feet. He arrived breathless to find the girls gathered in a sulky group.

'Ea! Come on—what are you gazing at, the audience asks for you again!'

'Oh, no it doesn't,' a tall blonde turned away rebelliously. 'They want the Carnation, and you'd better go and tell them she's forgotten the date, or overslept, or been murdered.'

'No, no—she is here—she is coming! I beg you, once more. What? Are you by any chance employed to take orders from me? Ah, that is better. Now then, please!'

Outside, Calcagno watched the cream coloured car zigzag towards him. There was something that was unfamiliar about it—it wasn't the Carnation's automobile at all. Yes, it was, it must be. Hope swallowed doubt, and then was shattered as the car came to a stop. Not her car at all, this one was smaller and the upholstery was green and not white. It contained also, now one came to look, an ex-king and his secretary.

'Good evening, your Majesty!' Calcagno forced a smile.

'Am I late?'

'No, your Majesty. The Carnation has not yet danced.'

There was nothing for it now; he would have to announce that the Carnation was indisposed, to accept that the gala night had ended in a fiasco.

During the intermission everyone was asking what had happened to the Carnation: she had been well yesterday, she had been at a supper party. Indisposed—could it be, was it possible . . . these rumours of yellow fever . . .

Billy Wykes, recently appointed engineer-in-chief of the San Roccan Grand Central Railway, pushed through the twittering crowd and for a handful of pink and yellow bank-notes purchased from the stage-doorkeeper the information that the Carnation's villa had been telephoned, and that she had left there more than an hour ago, bound for the theatre.

'And no one knows, save God, what has happened to her.'

The house, for the second half, was three-quarters full, but the most select, the most important patrons had not bothered to stay. Billy Wykes, after another fruitless visit to the stage door, trod out the twentieth cigarette of the evening, and with the nervous anxiety of a lover went off on foot. He swung jolting down the rough steps which intersected the motor road, and presently wound between high walls, Jesuit churches and shuttered shops. The hotel which he entered was small, but even if he could have afforded the Acropolis Hotel he had reasons for not staying there, and at any rate he had only booked his room for one night. The next day he would have to start off again with his collection of shabby travel-stained luggage for the encampment at rail-head, eighty miles away.

A few minutes after the engineer had marched off another cream and chromium car drew up in front of the theatre. The Carnation herself was at the wheel: she jumped out, left the door swinging, and ran past the doorkeeper into the astonished arms of Calcagno.

'Señorita! You are still alive! You are not dead? You are not even hurt?'

'I am still alive.' She detached herself from Calcagno. 'That is hardly so important as the gala night. What did you say? You sent them home?'

'Yes, yes, I said you were ill of a sudden. I made excuses —but you . . .' Calcagno's relief gave way to doubt and suspicion. She was very cool, in her white sports suit, with the beret clinging to her shiny black hair.

'I will tell you. Let us go into your office. You don't think I should let you down without good reason, do you?'

Calcagno led the way importantly, held the door for her, and then closed it and stood with his back against it.

'Get me some brandy. I've been so angry it has made me ill.' The Carnation threw off her beret, opened her jacket and breathed deeply. In the bright light he now saw that she was pale, and the hand that took the glass trembled.

'Thank you, Calcagno. Now I am a little less angry. Oh, but when I think of it! However, I will tell you. I left at the usual time—the car was waiting for me, and Enrique was in the driver's seat. At least, the man I thought was Enrique. We started off—I was thinking about nothing but my new dance—I didn't notice what turns we took, and at night all

15

the roads in the forest are the same as each other. The moment came, however, when I began to feel we had been driving for a very long time, and we were still in the forest. I looked at my watch—we should even then have been in the town, perhaps at the theatre. I wondered if Enrique had lost the way—it seemed impossible, for he has driven me a hundred times. I tapped on the glass—he did not turn round. I shouted to know if he was mad, or if he knew the time, or where we might be. Still he did not turn round— the car began to go faster. I opened the little window, and seized his shoulder—the man turned round—it was not Enrique at all—a man I had never seen, in the clothes of Enrique!'

'Ay! What a shock so terrible!' Calcagno took the glass, filled it and drained it himself.

'He smiled, said nothing, and picked up a revolver from his lap. What could I do? I thought, I am being kidnapped. That in itself did not frighten me—I think it is not the person who is kidnapped that pays the ransom, but the friends of that person. Or, if I was to be robbed, I had nothing—a ring, a few dollars, a little pin. But I thought all the time, I am late, they are waiting for me. One more mishap for the Acropolis.'

'Ah!' Calcagno was suddenly alert.

'What?'

'Nothing, nothing. Go on.'

'There is not much else. Now came the extraordinary thing. He stopped the car and jumped out. I had my hand on the catch of the other door to jump out the other side. I could run, I thought, as fast as I could. If he was alone, if there were no others hiding among the trees I could escape. But—' she spread her hands—'it was he who ran—straight into the forest and without looking back.'

'But—that was a bluff?'

'No—I don't know. He ran away—I waited—nothing happened. Suddenly I jumped into the driving seat and started the car. I drove for ten minutes as fast as I could. Then I stopped. It was a bad road in the forest—I did not know where. Bt there were stars. In Mexico I have ridden by the stars often. I turned the car and came back, driving quickly, ready to run down any one who tried to stop me. But there was no one—nothing! Nothing, except that I am not here to dance!'

Calcagno was striding up and down in a state of great agitation. The Carnation, for her part, was perfectly composed. She was a woman of astounding commonsense, astounding not because it was particularly sensible commonsense but because from her a temperament unreasonable and exaggerated would have been excused.

'It is very unheroic. If I had been bound and gagged—if I had been raped, then at least I should not have been made a fool of. The man was a small thief and he lost his nerve, I suppose. There is nothing to be done.'

'Nothing to be done?' Calcagno looked at her with bulbous eyes. 'Nothing to be done?' He snatched up the telephone.

'What are you doing now?'

He was answered before he could reply to her:

'Hullo? Yes—this is Calcagno. The Carnation is here— she is alive and unhurt, but ... What?' Calcagno visibly paled. 'Yes, I am here. I will wait. As quickly as possible, and tell no one.'

'Who is that you were speaking to?' she inquired.

'Penzuela. He is coming here. What a night is this! The house detective at the hotel has cleared out—vanished—'

'Well, what do we want with *him*?'

'With him? Nothing. But he has gone, and all the laundry at the hotel has been cut into ribbons!'

'Cut into ...' Her voice trailed off, and as she saw Calcagno's serious face she burst into laughter.

'Cut into ribbons,' he repeated. 'All the linen—twelve big hampers—every client will have to be compensated— and how is it to be explained? Now do you see—you are abducted—for what reason? So that you cannot dance—so that on a gala night the audience is disappointed. Hardly have we killed a false rumour that there is yellow fever in the hotel than the clean linen of every client is ruined. Yes —it is funny, it is a joke—they will not blame us. But they will go away and they will tell their friends, "In San Rocco there is a good theatre, but there may or there may not be a performance on any night. The hotel is good, but sometimes for a shirt you will be given a handful of ribbons. San Rocco is charming, but it is not a serious place, it is not civilized—it is without law."'

For Maître d'hôtel Penzuela, when he arrived, the Carnation's story was repeated. He was politely shocked, but he had his own troubles. The hotel, after all, was more important than the theatre. In the morning he would have to face a hundred angry patrons.

When everything had been said, and said twice, only one explanation remained: some person or persons were bent on ruining Pero Zaragoza and the Acropolis: the rumour of yellow fever, the abduction of the dancer, the sabotage of the linen, the disappearance of the house detective—bribed or intimidated—pointed only in that direction. Now many other slight mishaps in the past could be remembered— little things that had happened mysteriously, small things which accumulated to make bad publicity for 'the Athens of the Atlantic', 'the Lido of the West'.

Calcagno and Penzuela, badly shaken, nodded together: there was nothing for it but a cable to Zaragoza himself, now on his yearly visit to Europe in search of talent and to establish cordial relations with shipping companies and tourist agencies. Neither had wanted to be the first to suggest it, but once mentioned the idea had been seized upon with gladness and relief. Only the Carnation offered any criticism:

'Send for him to come back if you will, but what can he do more than anyone else?'The simple fact is, there has been a chain of misfortunes—a petty thief who loses his nerve, a laundry maid with a grudge against someone.'

But whatever simple conviction the Carnation may have expressed in the office she took not unreasonable precautions for her journey home. At her villa she was met with exclamations of relief and joy. Enrique, the chauffeur, had staggered in a few minutes before, dazed and half-articulate with a story of a mysterious attack. He had been preparing the car when he had received a blow on the head from an unseen assailant. She gave orders for his care, dismissed her bodyguard, and retired to her own room. She locked the door, and after a moment's hesitation, lifted the telephone receiver.

'Is that you, Billy?' she inquired presently in a voice which for him magically bridged an interval of four years. 'You shouldn't have come to the theatre,' she chided him, when her story had been told. 'You might have met Pero.'

'I wouldn't have gone out of my way to,' Wykes answered bitterly.

'He's not a bad sort of man,' the Carnation was pleading for herself too. 'Of course you hate him, but one can't help admiring him a little, if only he didn't look so comic.'

'I'm not interested in whether he's admirable, or what he looks like.'

'Very well, Billy,' the Carnation knew when to make her voice soft. 'And it doesn't matter, because he is in Europe, as it happens. Only now they talk of sending for him. I don't think he will be in a panic to return, but he may come back quicker than we hoped.'

The 'we' restored the young man at the other end to good humour:

'Go on talking, it's grand to hear your voice. I had begun to wonder if you really did still exist.'

'I do, Billy.'

'I want a little more proof still. Am I going to see you tonight?'

'Tonight? Well—tomorrow, perhaps.'

'Why not tonight?'

'You don't know the way here—'

'You can tell me.'

'Over the telephone?'

'What does it matter? Tomorrow I've got to go up to rail head—heaven knows when I shall have a chance of seeing you—perhaps not for weeks.'

The Carnation's objections were practical and not from the heart, and the heart won. Waiting in the darkness against the unbolted window she wondered how changed she would find the lover of four years ago, of her other life, and whether she would find it worth while to jeopardize all she now had for him. Calcagno and Penzuela, meanwhile, had despatched a cable to Pero Zaragoza, her discoverer and protector.


## CHAPTER 2

### PERO IN LONDON

Greek, Spaniard, Jew—Pero Zaragoza claimed a little from each race. He had been born in the Levant, but much of his life had been spent in the United States. That country, however, was too big for his loyalty—he was Old World at heart, a man of a close world, of a small island. In San Rocco he had found his spiritual home. His affinity in history was with the men of ancient or mediæval times who were so miscalled tyrants. Like them he was a devoted patron of the arts, and he looked as they probably did—swarthy, pot-bellied and undistinguished. He might have been a dictator, but he was a little soft and not ruthless enough for the present age. Instead, his kingdom was the Acropolis, a hotel, a cinema and a theatre. In the London hotel where he was staying he was respected for his riches, liked a little and laughed at a little. His appearance, as he rolled out of bed clutching the cable which had just been delivered, was more than a little comic. The elegant paisley pyjamas were too big for him and his dark hair, crossed in two tufts in front, suggesting the laureated head of one of the later of the Roman emperors. Shuffling into shoes of magenta and gold, he ran to the bedroom of his secretary, Hoffmann, who was still snoring.

The German closed his mouth, opened his eyes, saw his master, and sat up stiffly in bed. Pero thrust the cable into his hands, took a cigarette from the bedside table and went off on a journey for matches. Hoffmann scratched his shaven head, and looked at Pero phlegmatically.

'So!'

Pero pulled out the tray of the match-box, gathered up half a dozen at once from the carpet and jabbed them recklessly on the box. One day Hoffmann's cannon-fodder expression was going to rattle him.

'Pack,' he shot out. 'We go back by the next boat.'

Satisfied with the rapidity of his decision, Pero marched pompously back to his own room, and ordered coffee. Hoffmann rose, collected his dental plate, and lay down on the floor for his morning exercises.

Pero had meant to talk things over with Hoffmann, but the temptation of an arbitrary command had been too strong: vanity prevented him from reopening the subject. Of this Hoffmann, for his part, was perfectly aware, but when at last he was formally dressed, with a high white collar, he attended his master, and with the cable in his hand, observed:

'It appears the house detective has absconded?'

'Naturally. I never understood why you engaged him.'

'Every hotel must have a house detective.'

'But why a San Roccan? Of all nations they are the least trustworthy. I love San Rocco, it is my adopted country, but I should love it more if there were no San Roccans. I bring to the island visitors, and not visitors—but millionaires—I make San Rocco world known, and then they look at me, both the peasants and the caballeros, as if I did not exist.'

Hoffmann preserved a parade-ground silence.

'Very well. We shall take a detective back with us. An English detective, trustworthy and incorruptible. What other man could resist the temptations of the tropics?' Pero's voice purred: 'The palm trees, the bursting fruit, the flowers of a thousand colours, the women with—' He broke off: Hoffmann, anyway, knew the rest, Pero had dictated it to him the night before for a steamship handbook.

'Are our reservations booked?' he suddenly demanded.

'I go to do it.'

'You go to do it! Why haven't you done it! We leave

today. Find such a detective and engage him. Pay him well, and promise him a bonus of a thousand American dollars if he finds the saboteur—promise him five thousand!'

Hoffmann withdrew. Pero called him back:

'I want no publicity. Now I have told you everything. Let him meet us at the boat.'

Hoffmann returned to his room and started to organize his clothes for packing. He did not at once set about the engaging of a detective: Pero might change his mind, certainly burst in with another idea before long. In any case, their departure was sure to be delayed: Pero's business in Europe was only half done, he had many auditions, many interviews. Hoffmann's prediction proved partly right, for half an hour later Pero, still in his gaudy pyjamas, burst in waving the copy of an evening paper of the night before.

'Hoffmann, I have the exact man—Look!'

Pero was now mild and happy. He laid one hand on his secretary's shoulder and held the paper in front of him.

'I was looking in the advertisements for a detective agency, and see what I have found. Ex-Superintendent Simmonds, retired last week from Scotland Yard. Look—read ... the last of a famous group ... and see ... "In cooperation with the Spanish police, arrested the notorious share swindler, Zachary Hughes. He was then a young man, and this was his first big case, but there was no other Yard officer available with a knowledge of Spanish. A lion for work, he had studied three languages in his spare time."' Pero looked at Hoffmann with a soft smile: 'That is a thing we had not considered—that he should speak the language of San Rocco.'

The article was the usual newspaper write up, the re-shuffle of well-known cases inevitable whenever a Yard man of any importance is retired.

The ex-Superintendent was packing when the telephone rang in his Barons Court flat. He let it ring while he wrapped a pair of boots in newspaper.

'Is that ex-Superintendent Simmonds, please?' demanded Hoffmann, when he had been answered by an intimidatingly gruff 'Hullo'. 'Yes? I am speaking for Mr Zaragoza—'

22

'Who?'

'Mr Zaragoza—'

'Saratoga?'

'Zaragoza. He—'

'Never heard of him. What does he want?'

'Mr *Pero* Zaragoza. I am his secretary, and he wishes to know if you would kindly undertake a commission?'

'What sort of a commission? I can't say I'll undertake anything till I know what it is, can I?'

'No, no. That is clear. It is some detective work. It is—'

'I happen to have retired, and at the moment I'm busy.'

'Ah, but let me explain. It is urgent. You see—'

But whatever the stout superintendent was to see was not to be revealed on that occasion, for Simmonds was already on his way back to his packing.

Pero was at Hoffmann's elbow:

'He rang off.'

'Then ring him again, you fool. Ring again!'

Simmonds was consolidating the bottom layer with woollen vests when the telephone rang again.

'Oh, Mr Simmonds—'

This time the voice was not allowed to continue:

'Please tell Mr Saratoga that I am just going on a holiday for—for three years. I can't take on anything. Goodbye.'

Simmonds hung up, paused, then took up the telephone again:

'Ah, Miss—please don't put any calls through for half an hour. Thank you.'

Simmonds went almost as far as the Arabian adage 'It is better to sit than to stand, better to lie than to sit, better to die than to live.' This had to be reconciled with a life that had contained not much sitting and less than the normal amount of lying. As a consequence, now that his work was over, he was prepared to sit for the rest of his life. The 'lion for work' had hated work more than most people. Now he could vegetate. A bowler hat on his head, a cloth cap in his pocket, golf clubs which he would not use, one trunk and no responsibility—that was his plan for the next—he had said three years, well, he fixed no time limit. Vegetation without thought—he had done enough thinking for one lifetime, wrestled with enough problems. Thinking had always given him a headache; but then, when he did think he put more into thinking than most men, and in spite of the headaches more than most of the Big Five (or Four or Six, according to the whims of journalism). 'Blood pressure' had murmured a doctor, and prescribed 'diet': Simmonds had swallowed aspirins, opened his collar, put his head under the cold tap, and battled on. But now he was as near a nervous breakdown as a man can be and still look as healthy as a sergeant-major.

While Simmonds was entering a taxi, Pero was hurrying Hoffmann into another.

Simmonds sat back with his eyes half-closed—small blue resentful eyes, bloodshot, and with drooping pouches under them. He had banished thought. But thought has a habit of cropping up even when not wanted—and a thought loomed on his horizon that would have to be dealt with: he had forgotten to make arrangements for his she-kitten Mabel. The confounded telephone, the condemned Saratoga had put it out of his mind. There was nothing for it but to check the taxi, and turn back.

The taxi of Pero and Hoffmann arrived a moment after the taxi of Simmonds outside the block of flats. They went up, found the front door open, and Simmonds, bowler hatted, in his travelling coat of immemorial cut, on his knees enticing a tabby kitten from under the hat-stand. Pero pulled him by the shoulder, and, unabashed by two cold blue eyes, threw out an introduction and plunged into business, punctuating it only to send Hoffmann to pay off Simmond's taxi. When Hoffmann returned with the golf clubs and the valise, it had begun to dawn on Simmonds that the plump stranger took it for granted that he had agreed to travel across the Atlantic at a moment's notice to a pocket-sized republic, there to unravel a mystery of which he alone was worthy.

'You perhaps do not know the entertainment world, but you have heard of Deauville, of Biarritz, of the Lido, of the great wealth which is spent there. So is it spent in San

24

Rocco. But it is a gamble, the fashionable world is fickle. I have spent a million and a quarter dollars, it is essential nothing should happen to send away the wealthy persons who begin to come. If I start to go downhill, I go head over heels and I break my neck. I break the Republic of San Rocco, myself, my friend and secretary Hoffmann, here, and eleven hundred employees, not to speak of the artists, the dancers, the technicians and the impresarios I have under contract: with me would fall the Liberal government, and the President, Don Miguel, himself. That catastrophe must be prevented, and you alone can prevent it. Listen, Superintendent, three months ago San Rocco turned the corner: San Rocco at one bound became the most talked of resort in the Atlantic—"the Athens of the New World, the Jewel of the West Indies . . ."'

'"The Lido of the West,"' murmured Hoffmann.

'What?' Pero darted a look at the phlegmatic secretary, and then button-holed Simmonds again: 'Now funny things begin to happen. At first they can be ignored, but while one or two may be accidental, four or five can only happen by intention. It is impossible to say to my patrons, "Some unknown saboteur is at work." Soon it becomes said that the resort of San Rocco is not well conducted, it will become a joke and then an annoyance, and then they will not come, and then I am ruined. That is why, Mr Simmonds—,' Pero concluded with an appealing gesture—'I need your help, I demand your help, I implore you to come back with us.'

Simmonds, during the first part of this, had regarded Pero with the bewildered gaze of an ox in a butcher's advertisement, but during the course of it intelligence had returned to the small blue eyes and his features had been transformed by an expression of sagacity, a shrewdness that was sometimes only sly, sometimes almost noble. His professional conscience stirred; then he caught sight of his luggage and he broke away brusquely.

'I'm sorry, Mr Saratoga, but I'm just going away. I'm afraid I can't help you.'

'But you have no other engagement?'

'No.'

'Mr Simmonds, I am offering you five hundred American dollars a week and a bonus of five—of ten thousand dollars if you are successful. I pay all expenses, you have a suite in the hotel, you have tennis, dancing, the theatre, the bar—all free to you!'

'Sorry, I can't.' Simmonds began to collect his luggage together again. At mention of the money Hoffmann allowed himself to glance at the eighty pound a year flat with the faded curtains and the nineteen-hundred furniture. Pero inserted himself in front of Simmonds:

'Mr Simmonds, you have only to state your terms—I am rich, money is nothing to me. What may tempt you? San Rocco is the most beautiful island in the world. Bananas and oranges grow in the public streets, the climate is soft and warm, and the women—ah—'

'They're soft and warm too, I suppose?' Simmonds was heavily jovial. Hoffmann glanced at a photograph of Simmonds' married sister, taken in a studio at Clacton. But it was not this last inducement which had made Simmonds pause: it was simply curiosity, the routine curiosity of a policeman:

'Why, Mr Saratoga, may I ask, do you apply to me?'

Pero answered quite genuinely, although he was fully aware of the value of flattery:

'All over the world there is no man to be trusted like an English policeman. The San Roccan police—' he blew out his lips, 'and as for detectives from America, they are clever, but they can only work with machine guns and rubber tubes. This can only be solved by a man who is patient, by a man who is proof against temptation. In San Rocco everyone is corrupt, everyone takes bribes. You are only too proof against temptation. Listen then to the voice of duty, to your desire to help a fellow-man.'

Simmonds stroked his upper lip.

Pero held his breath for one moment, and then whipped out a cheque-book and wrote at speed but with a graceful flourishing hand a cheque for more money than Simmonds had ever possessed at one time before. He knew he had won, he wasn't going to spoil anything by more talk, the slip of paper he thrust upon Simmonds was more eloquent.

But it was not the money that persuaded Simmonds: a rebellious interest had overcome his misgivings. He said to himself: 'There's something fishy here.' He wouldn't have admitted it, but Pero's mercurial temperament had been too much for him, he had been twisted round the plump man's little finger. Actually, he hadn't said 'Yes', but he had taken the cheque, Hoffmann had told him the time of the boat, and Pero hadn't given him an opportunity to say 'No'. But it was a thoroughly bad-tempered and hard-put-upon superintendent who handed over Mabel to the grocer's wife, with gruff instructions for her care.

## CHAPTER 3

## THE FRIENDS OF MAN

The sun was low behind the hill-top cluster of white marble when Simmonds, in bowler hat and dark tweed suit, first trod the fertile soil of San Rocco. The sun twinkled on the brass-work of a prince's yacht and on the brass badges of the harbour officials. In the customs house the seams of his coat were stretched to bursting point as he stooped to open his luggage. First-class fare and the Arabian adage as a guiding rule had not improved his figure. But Hoffmann touched him on the elbow, and he looked up to see the chief official pocketing a roll of dollars. Pero's money opened magic doors everywhere, but the San Roccans regarded him coolly, with inscrutable reserve.

They drove first through dirty dock-side streets, no different from those of any harbour town, and then suddenly came into a wide square enclosed by low marble buildings from which flew the white and yellow flag of the republic. There was a fountain that did not play and iron gates that needed paint. Then the road mounted steeply and there were

27

glimpses of narrow alleys and of tall windowless buildings, of asses laden with water melons, merchandise or old fat women in black lace. All this was romance for the visitors to the Acropolis: their yachts in the harbour were suddenly disclosed almost perpendicularly below as the road hair-pinned out of the houses and slanted upwards through a belt of flowering shrubs. Then came the hotel entrance, modern and luxurious, and Maître d'hôtel Penzuela, defer-ential, cosmopolitan and, beside Pero, unimportant. It had already been decided that Simmonds should pass as Pero's new London agent, spending a few weeks in San Rocco. Penzuela had, of course, been expecting Pero, but the minor functionaries twittered with excitement: his return had been kept a secret. In Pero's private suite was waiting Saco, the olive-skinned valet, who looked exactly like an olive-skinned valet and nothing else.

'Well, Saco, you didn't expect me back so soon?' Pero yielded his panama and sat down in a scientifically con-structed metal chair which may have given him comfort but did not give him dignity.

'No, sir. Señor Penzuela told me this morning. I hope you have had a good trip.'

Pero indicated Simmonds:

'This is Señor Simmonds, my London manager. He will be here a few weeks, and you are to treat him exactly as if he were myself. Now show him to his room. We have dinner here.'

Simmonds, struggling with a black bow tie, regarded his big red face and his bristly moustache of reddish yellow hair in the peach-tinted mirrors with which his private bathroom was lined. A dilapidated shaving brush and an Oxo tin of efficient but unseductive tooth-powder stood on one of the glass shelves. His feet in patent leather pumps, which would have been serviceable hiking boots for some people, crushed the mat of sponge-rubber. He was out of place, and he didn't quite know what Pero expected of him. Pero, having once secured him, had been polite enough, but not very approach-able. He had said: 'Wait till we get to San Rocco.' Simmonds was quite willing to let events take their course. Blowing his nose and stepping high on the soft carpet, he emerged into the lounge. It was empty. He was crossing towards the window when there was a soft thud behind him. He swung round to face two large cat-like animals, the size of big dogs and of a uniform tawny colour. They stared at him, and he stared at them. Then the leaner of the two came forward and began to sniff his boots. Simmonds drew back his hand. The larger animal, uninterested, threw up a leg and started to wash.

'All right, pussy,' said Simmonds, 'I'm not going to hurt you. I have a pussy at home—But the point is,' he thought, 'is it going to hurt me?'

'Ah,' Pero had come in the door behind him, 'you are introducing yourself!'

'What are they?' Simmonds asked, gingerly touching one on the head. 'Small lions?'

'Yes, small lions—pumas, and my very good friends. This is Señora Sappho, and that is Señor Saturn.' Pero thrust out his arm, which Sappho took daintily between her teeth. Wrestling with it, he threw it over, and it lay on the carpet, revealing a creamy underside, thumping its tail in playful anger.

'They are quite harmless. They often sleep with me.' Pero was disarmingly simple. Simmonds qualified his opinion of Pero's character.

Saco came in with drinks, tall glasses of passion fruit juice, gin and crushed ice. Simmonds would have preferred a Bass. More and more he felt out of his element, in this bright, luxurious room which looked out over the Atlantic: a heavy, coolish breath laden with spicy scents came through the open window: lights were beginning to twinkle in the town. The two pumas were rolling together, and the untrustworthy looking manservant was emptying ash-trays. He began to be more and more certain that in this strange land, unbacked by the resources of the Yard, he was on a fool's errand. He cleared his throat, and was about to tell Pero his misgivings, when the door opened and a small figure in white rushed across the room into Pero's arms and kissed him on both cheeks with cries of pleasure and surprise.

'Pero, dearest, you never told me. I only just heard! I came immediately. Oh—' She caught sight of Simmonds.

Pero made the introduction: the Carnation gave Simmonds her hand, and he wrung it genially. A little astonished, her mouth opened in a merry smile. 'Not so dusty,' thought Simmonds. Then he remembered that he was a detective, and he took mental note that the girl seemed genuinely glad to see Pero. Saco came forward with a drink for her. Simmonds made another note: Saco's smile as he turned away was faintly cynical, the smile coinciding with an endearing phrase from the Carnation.

'Oh, Saco—' Pero stopped him— 'the señorita will dine with us. Set another place.'

'Oh, but I can't—' The Carnation's smile died away.

'No? You are dining with someone else?'

'Of course not, Pero. But I haven't changed—I came straight here as soon as I heard you were back—'

'No, no—' Pero signalled to Saco—'that does not matter.'

'I'm dirty and dusty.'

'You don't look it. You can have a bath here.'

'And get back into the same clothes?'

'I'll send for a new dress—'

'*Send* for a new dress! Pero, my angel, consider, one does not find a new dress as easily as that. No, no—it is more convenient for me to return home—there are things I want to do before I go to the theatre . . .'

All Pero's smiles had died, and the Carnation's excuses faded out as she saw his expression.

'You can telephone to your villa, or send Hoffmann on any errand you like. Because, you see, I have invited you to dinner.'

Simmonds was anxious to study the girl's face at that moment, but she had turned away to set down her glass. At any rate, the next moment she was chattering brightly.

As dinner was served Hoffmann entered, clicked his heels and bent deferentially over her hand. He had something to impart to Pero, and they spoke in more rapid Spanish than Simmonds could follow. The Carnation, who had been momentarily brooding, suddenly opened her eyes at him.

'This is your first visit to San Rocco?'

'Yes.'

'You are Pero's London agent? I wonder what he requires an agent in London for?'

Simmonds preserved his good humour, but it took a cleverer girl than the Carnation to pump him.

'The question is, what is the London agent doing in San Rocco? Well, of course, I've come to see if everything I've heard about you is true.'

'And is it?'

'Oh, give me a chance!'

She appreciated him with wide eyes. Then the subject was changed by the entry of the two pumas, who had followed Saco into the room with the fish.

'Sappho, Saturn!' She pushed back her chair and extended her arms towards them. Sappho butted her thigh gently.

'Señor Saratoga is very fond of them,' said Simmonds conversationally.

'Oh yes. He loves them.'

'How long has he had them?'

'Four years. A friend in Brazil gave them him when he was there. Oh, but you should see him driving with them sometimes in his two-seater. They wear collars when they go out, and he brings them to see me.'

'Aren't they dangerous—if they don't like anyone?' Simmonds remembered the story of the pet tiger which licked its master's hand till it drew blood. The story had spoiled a childish hope, and tigers as pets had been barred.

'Dangerous? These? But don't you know, they are called "the Friends of Man"? They follow men in the jungle only for the pleasure of their company. I have heard they make pets of men, as men make pets of cats.'

'Do you think they'll make a pet of me?' Simmonds inquired facetiously. He was getting on with the Carnation, that was clear.

'They say,' she continued, 'that pumas weep tears when the men shoot them.'

'Well, then, why do men shoot them?'

'Why do men do cruel things?' The Carnation looked at

him with a sincere brow. 'When men are afraid, then they do cruel things.'

This excellent truth Simmonds received with a sagacious nod. Pero broke into the conversation and for the rest of the meal Simmonds was silent while the technicalities of theatrical production was discussed. Once the Carnation—on purpose?—asked what the London agent considered best, but Pero deftly steered the conversation into a different channel. The meal was hurried, and the Carnation departed swiftly for the theatre. Pero went with her to the door, leaving Hoffmann and Simmonds together.

'She has a very great talent,' Hoffmann said heavily. 'She has the combination of brains and beauty that will make a world star. If she is not one already. She has been twice offered contracts by Hollywood, and from Paris and New York offers come always.'

'But she prefers to stay in San Rocco?' Simmonds inquired, sharply but not too sharply.

'She is happy here.'

'And I suppose she is under contract to Señor Sara—Zaragoza?' He had got the name right at last.

'No, there is nothing formal. But she owes everything to him.'

'And is staying here out of gratitude?' wondered Simmonds to himself. He made a mental note that the Carnation's reasons for refusing world fame must be studied. He didn't believe that it was for love of Pero, and he wasn't sure that Pero himself thought so. Pero hadn't revealed that he was a detective, but that would have to come out sooner or later, since it was part of his job to solve the mystery of her abduction—or rather, now he came to think of it, of the fact that she had been late for the gala performance, and that her chauffeur had been sandbagged.

Thinking it over, Simmonds judged that Pero wouldn't have brought him to San Rocco unless he had suspected that the unknown saboteur might be among his intimates. To track down an outsider would require not one man, but an organization.

# CHAPTER 4

## THE FRIENDS OF WOMEN

When Simmonds accompanied Pero to the theatre that night he made no reference to the Carnation. Pero was abstracted and not too genial, and Simmonds was ready to accept for the moment that the girl was not to be let into his secret. No doubt in good time Pero would tell him what he had to do, and how he was to set about his job, and in the meantime he was getting good money. Simmonds did not shirk either work or responsibility, but he didn't go about looking for it. He didn't mind waiting for Pero to say the word go.

The foyer buzzed with people. Many greeted Pero and he was as affable as a head waiter in return. The other side of the picture was the deference shown by Calcagno, the manager, and assistants and officials, who were on their toes at the unexpected return of their employer. Hoffmann hovered near, as punctilious and reserved as ever. Pero bowed and smiled to a grey-haired American with two sulky American daughters, and turned to Hoffmann without any smile and said:

'You can take Mr Simmonds in. I shall be in the office with Calcagno.'

Hoffmann listened, but he had been watchfully eyeing the door, and now he directed Pero's attention towards it:

'Sir—his Excellency!'

Four or five gentlemen with ribbons and orders had made a lane through the crowd, and after them appeared Don Miguel, tall, mild and undecorated: on his arm there was a middle-aged woman, expensively but not successfully dressed, a woman with prominent dark eyes and an energetic personality. It was she who spotted Pero, and with an exclamation of pleasure drew her husband in that direction.

Spanish courtesies over, Simmonds was introduced. Don Miguel gave him a thin hand and a charming smile.

'I am glad to see you. I hope you had a good journey, and that you will enjoy your stay in San Rocco.'

Carlotta de Valuque did not allow Simmonds to reply to this formula of welcome, her whole eager personality had been projected towards him as soon as she heard that he was English.

'I've been in London, Mr Simmonds,' she said proudly in English, her lips, full and slightly moustached, parting over white teeth. 'I'm very glad to meet an Englishman here. I have an English automobile and an English chauffeur. You must come to the Palace for afternoon tea.'

'Thank you, Madam—your Excellency.' Simmonds was not a snob, but he didn't mind feeling important.

'I want to have a long talk with you. We read all the papers, but I believe in first-hand knowledge whenever it is possible. Now take your political situation for instance—'

Don Miguel decided to come to the rescue of the bewildered Simmonds:

'Lotta, in England they do not have political situations. But Mr Simmonds shall tell you exactly how they don't have them,' he added hastily, at a glance from his wife. 'Yes, certainly—and now . . .' He made a movement towards the grand staircase. Carlotta accepted her husband's lead—but only because they are in public, thought Simmonds—and turned to go with a friendly smile. Don Miguel looked back towards Simmonds with a glance that was now quite blank, but that would have contained, if it had contained anything, an apology and a philosophy of life.

Simmonds liked the president.

The curtain was already up when Hoffmann and Simmonds took their seats at the end of a row and at the back. The various novelties of the day had made the superintendent sleepy, and through almost closed eyelids he watched the movements of the chorus, the Japanese acrobats, the Russian ballet, the American stock-whip expert and all the other varieties of Pero's international programme: which was not, however, international enough for Simmonds, whose taste was for Gracie Fields and Tom Walls. He had almost entirely dozed off when Hoffmann whispered gutturally:

'Now see, the Carnation!'

Simmonds opened his eyes: the expectant silence of the audience told him that he ought to be impressed, but at first he wasn't roused to any great heights of enthusiasm. The girl was sure of herself, certainly, and she looked smart and neat in a simple white costume—she always wore white. Her movements at first were hesitating and eccentric, the music thin and broken, but as the pace worked up, the strange, slipshod steps, repeated at speed, revealed a pattern, complicated and elusive, but evidently meant to be something.

'Wunderbar, wunderbar!' Hoffmann was exclaiming at intervals.

'Nice legs,' Simmonds admitted. A small exclamation at his elbow made him look round: Pero was standing in the gangway just behind, and his face was transfigured: it was the face of a worshipper, ecstatic and uplifted.

The old wardrobe mistress with the black moustache sat in a chair of raw hide and chromium-plated tubes, sewing patiently at a pair of silk fleshings. The chair had been borrowed from the property master, and the fleshings belonged to Dora, of Nora and Dora, the English Twins. The grapes which she crushed with her leathery tongue and swallowed whole came from the garden of her son-in-law up in the hills. The interval had come and gone: the fleshings wouldn't be required until tomorrow, but she might as well sew as sit idly waiting to take charge of the costumes at the end of the show. Presently she began to cough: taking her hooked nose between her fingers she looked round about, saw a newspaper on the floor, and blew and expectorated neatly into it. No one could find fault with her manners. But the tickling at the back of her throat continued, and looking up she saw a thin blueish haze between herself and the naked electric bulb. With deliberation she stuck the needle in the bosom of her dress, folded the fleshings over the back of the chair, and hobbled towards the sewing-room, outside of which she had been sitting. Some careless girl must have left the electric iron on the ironing cloth and forgotten to switch it off: they were always borrowing it for their stockings and underclothes, strictly against the rules. They would get old Mother Luisa into trouble one of these days, but that was a thing they did not think of. But no, the iron was cold: yet, undoubtedly, something was burning somewhere. The old woman sniffed around, opened a closet, and looked up towards the ceiling. Then, kilting her skirts, she mounted the iron ladder which led to the store-room above. Yes, undoubtedly there was a fire here. Under the locked door curled ringlets of smoke. There was a fire alarm two feet away, but there was a glass which had to be broken, and old Mother Luisa no more thought of breaking the glass than of battering down the store-room door.

On her way to Paulo, the stage-doorkeeper and her crony, she passed José, the fireman, in his smart white drill uniform with the gold chain epaulets. She was not on good terms with the fireman, who had once complained of her sleeping, it was after a party, all one night in the orchestra pit. And also he was a smart young man who had spent many years in Chicago, and therefore to be suspected and despised by a true San Roccan. So old Mother Luisa hobbled to the stage-doorkeeper, and to him, after passing the time of day, reported the fire in the store-room. Paulo searched in a drawer of odds and ends for his steel-rimmed spectacles, and accompanied Mother Luisa towards the wardrobe. Yes, they both agreed, the store-room was certainly on fire.

'That is very dangerous, Mother, because the room is full of costumes, and once they start burning there is likely to be a serious fire.'

'The door is locked.'

'Certainly it is. I have one key, and Señor Calcagno has the other. I cannot unlock it alone. Perhaps we should tell José? After all, he is the fireman, and it is his responsibility.'

'Then you tell him. For myself, I do not like to do him the favour.'

By the time Paulo had returned with the young fireman

the smoke was pouring out in earnest, passers-by had begun to collect, and José realized that some spectacular action was required to justify his golden epaulets. Sending Paulo to fetch the manager, he attacked the door with his axe. Smoke bellying through the broken panels sent them all choking backwards. The draught brought to life the smouldering cloth, and a sheet of flame roared towards them. Two stage hands arriving with extinguishers dropped them and fled, bowling over a couple of ballet dancers who had run up at that moment. Mother Luisa ran along the passage screaming, 'Fire! Fire!' Newcomers rushed forward, and those near the fire struggled back, the smoke overtook them, and there was a general panic. Volunteer firemen struggled with the hydrant, girls appeared at the doors of their dressing-rooms, screamed, and ran back for clothes. It occurred to one of them to rush past the wings spreading the alarm: those on the stage caught the infection, the line of arms and hips wavered, and broke up in confusion. Someone in the audience caught the terrible word and started to scramble out. At this moment Calcagno, fetched by the stage-doorkeeper, appeared before the safety curtain which had come down with a rush. Simmonds, running after Pero, heard the beginning of Calcagno's appeal for calm. It must have succeeded because as he hurried down back passages he heard the orchestra strike up again. Pero tore a door open, but was swept back into the arms of Simmonds by a riot of young women.

'Terrible, terrible,' he moaned, 'the fire spreads, everything goes, I shall be ruined. You've come too late—too late!'

'Well, where's the fire?' Simmonds shook Pero free, and made for the door. On the other side the passage was empty. He ran down it, and was soon lost in a maze of small passages, all deserted. He had no clear idea of the plan of the building, which was eccentric, as it had been built to fit the contours of the hill. Concrete steps led up and then down, doors led to dark rooms, coal holes, stores, charwomen's cubby holes. Simmonds pulled up, wondered whether to retrace his steps, and then saw a door which obviously led to the open air. To go through this and to start again seemed the quickest plan. Outside, an iron ladder led up again to the second storey. Hoping that it would bring him to the scene of the fire, Simmonds hurried up it. At the top was another door, and only after having passed through it did Simmonds realize a strange thing: the door was an emergency exit, without a handle on the outside. Inside there was the usual patent push-bar, so that it was easy to leave the theatre through it, but normally impossible to enter. Yet he had entered, the door must have been ajar, and it was the type of door which is canted to close automatically. Simmonds pulled out the pocket torch, his only weapon, and played it up and down. The door had swung to after him, but there was a crack a couple of inches wide. Suddenly he stooped: the door was prevented from closing by a small piece of wood. Well, somebody must have put the wood in that place, and there could only be one reason: to allow someone else to enter the theatre in an unauthorized manner.

It was something to be investigated later: at the moment he was trying to find the fire. He was now in a short corridor, from which opened several doors. It was empty, no crowds, no panic. Faintly, he could hear the orchestra—evidently the theatre was in no great danger, certainly wasn't being evacuated. One door was as good as another, and he tried the first: the room into which he stepped was dark: his pocket torch showed up a bath, and the pencil of light sprang back at him from a dozen directions. Evidently a star's bathroom, lined with mirrors. He was about to step forward when from an adjoining room he heard the rapid opening and closing of a door, and a quick exclamation in a woman's voice. The Carnation's voice. On tiptoe Simmonds proceeded with the silent tread peculiar to himself towards the dividing door. With the most complete muscle control he turned the knob.

His habit was suspicion, and the fire exit had been tampered with. An inch crack was sufficient for him to see the Carnation, in negligée, and a tall, youngish man who was embracing her passionately. They parted at that moment, the Carnation pushing him away with a hasty glance at the door through which he had come.

'Billy—be careful. Pero's back! He came back tonight.'

'I waited for you—'

'Yes, yes—he made me have dinner with him. I couldn't escape even to send a message.'

'Well, look here, what are we to do?'

'Nothing now, nothing. You must go. There's been a fire —I slipped up here, but he'll be coming after me, to see if I'm all right. Listen—' She grabbed the young man, the young Englishman, by the arm. Footsteps were heard in the passage. 'Through the bathroom!' She pushed him towards the door against which Simmonds was listening. Simmonds just had time to fold himself against the wall. The young man fumbled his way across the room and slipped out through the door on the other side, and then the Carnation's door burst open again, and Pero could be heard, joyful at having found her unharmed.

'But is it serious, is there any danger?' she demanded.

'No, no, I don't think so. There is a lot of smoke, I can't tell. Some people have been hurt, but the audience is going out quietly.'

Simmonds was going out quietly too. The fire might or might not be important: he was rather more interested in his discovery of one reason at least why the Carnation might prefer San Rocco to the fame and money of either continent.


CHAPTER 5

WHAT HAPPENED IN PRINKIPO


Simmonds's starched shirt was limp by the time, making a second entry into the theatre and a more lucky one, he had reached the wardrobe store-room. The approach was packed with curious spectators, who had regained their courage on seeing that the fire was not dangerous: they stood about in every sort of costume, and from the adjoining dressing-room of the chorus chairs had been brought so that even late-comers might have a good view. The air reeked with the smell of burning cloth and feathers, pieces of charred cloth floated by, smudging walls and faces, and underfoot were puddles of water and the dirty yellow foam of the fire extinguishers.

Simmonds forced his way through to the front: he saw the broken door which hung on one hinge, and the blackened shell of the store-room, over which played the fireman's bullseye. There was no window, and the electric bulb had been melted in the fire. José and two other inferior firemen were stamping out the last embers, pulling bundles of reeking costumes from the gutted shelves and treading everything into a syrupy mess on the floor. Then he caught sight of Hoffman and Calcagno, who were questioning old Mother Luisa. Simmonds could follow the questions, but not the answers, for the old woman's brand of Spanish was not one which Simmonds could follow. He placed himself at Hoffmann's side.

'And you were sitting by this door all evening, and you saw no one enter?'

Mother Luisa answered volubly.

'What does she say?' whispered Simmonds.

'She says she was here since five o'clock, in the sewing-room or just outside, and no stranger came near. But then we know that the door was double-locked.'

'Ask her when it was last unlocked.'

People were now beginning to stare at Simmonds. Hoffmann put the question. The old woman looked at Simmonds with her witch's eye, and spoke rapidly.

'A friend of Señor Zaragoza's,' explained Hoffmann briefly, and then, interpreting the old woman, 'No one has entered this room for two days. Some of these costumes, especially those with the ostrich feathers, are very valuable, and the key must be fetched from Señor Calcagno. The assistant stage-manager checks what is taken. But the costumes stored here are those not in immediate use.'

40

While Hoffmann had been talking a private argument had sprung up between the old woman and José the fireman, in which some of the surrounding workmen and volunteer firemen took sides.

Simmonds scratched the back of his head. In this babel he couldn't do anything. For one thing, he had no authority, the only one there who understood his position was Hoffmann. This was a thing for the San Roccan police, not for him. His duties, he felt, were more discreet, more intimate —at least he imagined that was Pero's intention. The fire, of course, might have been accidental, some sort of spontaneous combustion. At all events, for him to use the normal detective methods was useless. There was one thing this fire might do, it might make Pero come down to brass tacks.

'Why don't you call in the police?' he asked Hoffmann shortly.

'Oh, one would have to ask Señor Zaragoza about that.'

'Then why don't you ask him?'

Hoffmann stared round mistily, as if looking for Pero.

'The police,' he added, 'do not come up the hill.'

'Up the hill?'

'To the Acropolis. It's all private property, and anyway . . . however, we must ask Señor Zaragoza.'

'Anyway, what?' demanded Simmonds. Hoffmann looked at him impassively, but was saved from answering by the arrival of Pero himself. The crowd gave way, and there was immediate silence as Pero trotted up, distracted and anxious. He took Simmonds's arm:

'There is nothing to be done here—I have been to see if the Carnation was safe and unhurt. And what happened to you?'

'I've been looking round, but if you want me to . . .'

'Good,' Pero broke in, flustered and incapable of hearing him out. 'Now, José, you,' he turned abruptly, 'send everyone away, and stay on guard here. Nothing is to be touched. There will be an investigation in the morning.'

Simmonds found himself being led away, Hoffmann trailing behind them.

'But, Mr Zaragoza, tonight—'

'Tonight I am too nervous to think, to begin to think. You see, I am six hours back, and the saboteur has begun again. It is only by good chance that the whole theatre has not been burned to the ground, and perhaps the hotel too.'

'Are you insured?' Simmonds suddenly asked.

'Insured?' Pero laughed. 'Certainly the fabric is insured, but that is nothing. It is the good-will—things are beginning to go now. Suppose there is a big fire, then it will take two years to rebuild—all my talent is dispersed, I make no money in the meantime, I must start again. I should not have the heart.'

They were now walking by the private way to Pero's apartments. They continued in silence. It had naturally passed through Simmonds's suspicious mind that Pero himself might have instigated the fire: there was certainly something a little strange in his behaviour: but his declaration that insurance could not cover the loss in this case did seem reasonable.

'Ah!' Pero let out a sigh of relief as he reached his own room, entered quickly and closed the door. He looked at Simmonds with a smile, an engaging, quizzical smile which dispersed all suspicions, a smile which was, if Simmonds but knew it, his chief asset in business. And yet a genuine smile.

'I am not a very brave man, Mr Simmonds,' he explained sweetly. 'All the time we were walking here I was wondering if there is an assassin in wait for me. I do not know if anyone wishes to kill me, but if they wish to ruin me, then they may also wish to kill me.'

'But you don't know of anyone?' Simmonds asked.

'Hoffmann—if you please.' Pero indicated the bell. Simmonds repeated his question. Pero nervously lit a cigarette. Then the question, apparently, arrived.

'What? Do I know of anyone? Now, if I did, I should tell you, and I shouldn't have brought you here?'

That seemed logical, but it seemed to Simmonds as if a different answer had been considered and rejected during the moment when the match was being struck.

Saco came in. Simmonds had not heard him enter, and

as Pero spoke, ordering drinks, he swung round. He did not like people who walked so silently, not even when it was their profession to be unobtrusive. The olive face was already turned half away, but Simmonds had a fleeting impression of a black smut across one temple.

'Hey—wait a moment—' Saco paused. 'May I have—' Simmonds included Pero too, but kept his eye on Saco— 'may I have a cup of tea?'

It was an excuse to delay Saco, but also it was just exactly what he did want.

Yes, there was a definite black smut.

'Watching fires is thirsty work,' Simmonds explained casually, with a smile for Saco, 'and there's nothing like tea if you're thirsty.'

'Yes, sir. I heard there had been a fire. Señor Penzuela warned us all here.'

'But it wasn't much of a one, was it?'

'I am glad to hear that, sir.'

Simmonds relaxed, indifferently. Unwise to put Saco on his guard, if there was anything wrong with Saco. After all, a smut might be acquired in a thousand ways, even if he had played truant and 'gone to see the fire' that did not make him guilty. And Simmonds always stoutly refused to be led astray by personal antipathies. However, when Saco had gone, he asked Pero directly:

'How long has that man been with you?'

'Saco? Oh, many years.'

'Well, now, you see, Mr Zaragoza,' Simmonds began to get down to business, 'it's time you told me exactly how you want me to carry on. I'm willing to do anything. But take this fire, for instance, if I'm to get busy on that I've got to have public authority to question people. Of course I understand that once it's known that I'm a detective, I'm not so useful, in some ways. But I don't quite understand yet how you expect me to be useful. If you don't mind me saying so, you . . .'

The buzz of the telephone broke into Simmonds's complaint. Hoffmann, who was nearest to it, picked up the receiver. But Pero had jumped up with outstretched hand.

'I'll answer it!'

One end of a brief conversation could be heard, and then Pero put down the receiver.

'Devil! It's the president—his adjutant wants me to go down, I've been asked for. His Excellency is in the supper-room. Confound him!' This was to Hoffmann. Then he turned to Simmonds: 'After all, I am a maître d'hôtel, hey? I must go and be pleasant. Tomorrow, perhaps, we will have a little talk?'

'Yes.'

Pero, at the door, seemed to be waiting for Simmonds to go.

'You will perhaps wish to go to your room?'

'Oh, thanks. I'll just wait for my tea, then I'll go along.'

'Oh, but certainly, certainly. Then—I wish you good night.'

'Good night.'

Hoffmann followed Pero out. Simmonds sat and cogitated on several matters, and then Saco came in with the tray of drinks, and the tea for Simmonds. There was no smut this time. Saco arranged the tea-things in a loaded silence, let his hands fall away, hesitated, seeing that everything was right, and then snatched up the milk jug.

'Tch! I will fetch some more—a little cinder. They have been blowing in through the window, from the fire, one supposes.'

'Yes, I noticed you had got some on your face.'

Volunteered excuses are pointers to an uneasy conscience, that was rule number three, but Simmonds was too lazy to pursue the idea, and when Saco came back with fresh milk there was something else to occupy his attention, for with Saco came the two pumas. Catlike, they kept their eye on him, but approached indirectly and by way of various pieces of furniture. The she-puma stood suddenly and washed her chest, which may have needed washing, but was, one suspected, the easiest place to wash while she kept an eye on the stranger.

'Señor Zaragoza is having them in his bedroom tonight,' Saco said.

'Oh. Watch-dogs, or what?'

'Oh, they are a great protection.'

Saco answered with a smile which said, 'We all know about that,' and then crossing to the farther room clicked his tongue encouragingly. The cats proceeded, treading high and with waving tails, to Pero's bedroom, and Saco closed the door on them. Simmonds let Saco go. At that moment he was feeling disgruntled and despondent. The trip across the Atlantic was a fool's errand. Perhaps, after all, he was getting too old for his job.

The hot tea was gratifying, but the silver pot was a little one, and two small cups were nothing to Simmonds. He looked round for the bell, and seeing a bell-push on the writing-table, against which Pero had been sitting, he pressed it. The telephone buzzed. The clerk, presumably at the hotel switchboard, asked what number he wanted.

'I don't want a number. Didn't you ring me?'

'No, sir. No call for you.'

'Oh. Well, the bell rang.'

Simmonds put back the receiver, and then paused in thought. Remembering certain things, he touched the bell-push on Pero's desk once more. The telephone buzzed. This time Simmonds did not touch it.

'Ho, ho,' he thought to himself, 'so that was Pero's little game, was it? He didn't want to answer me, so he faked a telephone call. Now, why did he do that?'

To make sure of his facts, Simmonds decided to go down to the supper-room. If Pero wasn't there, if His Excellency wasn't there, he would have something to think about.

A short corridor led from the private suite to one of the main arteries of the hotel. Simmonds pressed the lift bell and waited. From afar came distant sounds of music. A floor waiter passed with an ice bucket, and then a festive party of Americans. The lift sprang up, and the bronze grille flew open.

'Which floor, sir?' asked the dusky lift-boy in the silver uniform, speaking in English.

'Now, how on earth did he know I was English?' Simmonds thought, studying his image in the mirrored lift.

'I want the supper-room, Sonny.'

On the ground floor, music suggested the direction: Simmonds drifted towards it, fingering in his pocket the gold pass which Pero had given him. This was a plain gold disc, with the monogram PZ engraved on one side: there were only, Pero had said, a dozen in existence, and it allowed the owner to go anywhere and order anything in Pero's kingdom.

The room was hot and noisy, a string band wailed and the dance-floor was packed—lovely women, wealthy visitors, Spanish gentlemen from the island, officers from the warship in the harbour, officials, Jews, some girls from the theatre, and, Simmonds could see when he had got his bearings, the presidential party. So perhaps Pero had been called down after all, for he was sitting there opposite his languid and dreamy Excellency, with the Carnation on one side, and the president's wife on the other. That woman was talking energetically, and the Carnation in looking round met Simmonds's eyes. She smiled sympathetically, and looked away, but when he looked back he caught her glancing in his direction again with an expression that was interested and perhaps slightly anxious. She acknowledged him with a flicker of her eyes, and after a quick glance at the rest of the party—Pero and the President's wife were talking together, and the President was absorbed in day-dreams—she gestured that she was coming to join him.

Simmonds mentally raised his eyebrows: the girl had been friendly at dinner, but only, he imagined, because she was a normally polite person, and she had been sitting next to him. The stares of half the room followed her as she made her way round, sheathed in white, with a spray of waxy white flowers tumbling from her shoulder to her waist.

'I saw you were alone,' she said showing white teeth, 'the others are talking, and I'm tired and I don't want to dance. And I want to sit here, because you don't want to dance either.'

'How do you know I don't want to dance?' asked Simmonds, remembering that he had forgotten to stand up at

46

her approach, and bobbing up now as the Carnation was assisted to sit down by one of three waiters who hurried forward.

'Because—' she waited for the men to withdraw—'because you are an observer. Have you picked out the criminal yet?'

She laughed elegantly at his momentary reaction.

'Pero told me why you are here,' she continued, 'and I want to know what you have found out.'

'Oh.' When Simmonds was taken aback he refrained from speaking.

'Perhaps you don't want to tell me? Or perhaps you haven't found out anything? Of course, you've only been here a few hours.'

'That is so,' he answered good humouredly.

'Oh, you're putting me off with soft answers,' she dropped him a melting look, 'but you can tell me, because anything you tell Pero, I shall get to know.'

'Well, when I've got something to tell Pero . . .'

'Then you haven't anything, yet?' The demand came quickly. He estimated her:

'Not very much.'

'But something?'

'Oh, yes. Something.' She might have large brown eyes, but Simmonds's were small and blue and keen. 'I've been getting my bearings,' he continued, looking at her. 'It's a funny sort of a place, this: all sorts of people, if you know what I mean. But not many Englishmen.'

The young girl replied with unconcern:

'No, not many Englishmen, certainly.'

'I suppose I'm the only one here tonight, for instance?'

'I expect so.'

She looked at him steadily, inquiringly, and Simmonds discharged his shot:

'Do you know any—Englishmen, I mean—here?'

'Oh, yes . . . several. There's the English consul, and there are some railway engineers.'

'Oh, ah, friends of Mr Saratoga, I suppose?' He could be casual too.

'No—' she chose her words—'not particularly friends of Pero.'

Simmonds relaxed and offered her a cigarette. He had meant his probing to be transparent, in the hopes that she would talk. She was still, he could see, wondering how he knew about her own particular Englishman, or if he did know. It had also been a little vanity on his part to let her see that he was not such a fool as he looked, or as he was often afraid that he did look.

'It's funny, you know,' he continued, 'Mr Zaragoza insisted on my coming here, and it's costing him quite a lot of money, but he doesn't *tell* me anything. I mean, this fire and the other things, he must have some idea who is at the back of them. All he says is—he hasn't got an enemy. But you can't tell me that a man like Mr Zaragoza can knock about the world for forty years, piling up his millions, without running foul of someone who'd like to put him down.'

Simmonds had been quite loquacious and finally indignant. The Carnation looked at him with big eyes, and answered briefly:

'But I *don't* tell you such a thing.'

'What?'

'If Pero told you that he had no enemies in the world, then he must have a short memory. Ask him what happened in Prinkipo, ten years ago. Or ask Hoffmann.'


## CHAPTER 6

## THE THREE UNKNOWNS


Simmonds timed his departure from the supper-room so as to be waiting for Pero as Pero and Hoffmann approached the private suite.

'So you did not go to bed after all,' said Pero, as Simmonds followed him into the room. 'The good Carlotta was taking up all my attention, or I would have seen that you had a partner to dance with.'

'I don't dance.'

'No? I admit, at our age, my friend, one is content to watch.'

'I think that I am going to bed,' Hoffmann observed hopefully, from the doorway.

'Oh, yes, we are all going to bed now. Good night. And good night, Mr Simmonds.'

'Excuse me—' Simmonds was planted firmly in the room —'may I have a few words with you?'

While Pero was hesitating, Simmonds closed the door and sat down.

'Mr Zaragoza, I was told to ask you a question.'

'Yes?'

'I was told to ask you what happened in Prinkipo, ten years ago.'

'*In* Prinkipo? Oh, yes, that was the Carnation. I told her you were a detective. She would have found out in any case, she has very sharp eyes, that girl. Not that there is any reason why she should not know.'

'What *did* happen, Mr Zaragoza?'

Pero made the gesture of a man who has decided to explain everything.

'Mr Simmonds, you shall be told. I hoped that it would not be necessary for me to go into the past. But now I must, or you will have no confidence in me. That is so? Very well. The story I have to tell you is not greatly to my credit. I regret it. But great men have sometimes to be unscrupulous, in politics as in business. Examine the life of any world figure—but no, it is not history, but my history you wish to hear.'

Pero stood up and started to walk up and down.

'After the great world war,' he continued, 'you may remember that fighting went on in Asia Minor for a number of years, until Mustafa Kemal despatched the Greeks from Smyrna. At that time I found myself in the Levant—I was born there, and I had returned, because my father had died,

49

and there was some property to sell. It was then that I first became interested in the entertainment business—I saw all those people who were tired of the war and its horrors. I had first a little cinema in Salonika, and then I had a circuit of cinemas—in Cairo, in Algeria, oh, in twelve or thirteen places. I made a good deal of money, and I already had Hoffmann to work for me—he was a German officer who had been left behind by the war. Now I determined to make even more money, and I built a little casino in Tunis—dancing, gambling, cabaret—ah, it was a time for making money. All that time I was travelling, travelling, in little steamers, in bad trains. I had no time to live, to enjoy myself, and all the time my father's little house in Corinth was waiting. I thought I had reached the height of my ambition, I thought I would retire and leave my business in the hands of capable managers. Now those who knew of my interests offered me a site in Istanbul which was suitable for a little casino, a little theatre. I declined—for reasons which are unessential. But presently I received a letter from my agent suggesting I should advance the money to an independent company. I lent the money, and the casino was built. It was called the Prinkipo, because from the terrace there was a view of the islands of Prinkipo, where wealthy Turks and Christians have their villas. And at that moment came a change in politics, Turkey became progressive, there was much talk of culture, and the theatre attached to the casino began to make money. I determined to buy out the independent company and to receive the full profits, instead of the small fixed interest. They refused to sell; I called in my capital, hoping it would break them, but they found more. Then it occurred to me that if only for a short time their business was to decline, I could buy at my own price. So, Mr Simmonds, I set to work to make that business decline. There was a rumour about spotted fever, there was a time,' Pero murmured reflectively, 'when the theatre was nearly burned down.'

'Ah!'

'Yes, I do not have to tell you that what is happening here in San Rocco happened, in more or less the same way, there. But do not blame me too much. I had left it to my agents, offering them money if they could buy the theatre for me, suggesting, perhaps, a little whispering campaign. Only afterwards did I learn of the things that had been done. But I am not so small that I cannot accept responsibility.'

Simmonds nodded: the man was a scoundrel, but he was not small.

'So,' continued Pero, 'the independent company was broken, but at that time after all I did not buy it up, because I had an offer from New York, and shortly afterwards I left the Levant.'

'So,' Simmonds summed up briskly, 'you think that the people you broke are taking their revenge on you?'

'It is the only explanation.'

'Then it doesn't seem a very difficult case. As soon as one of them shows up here, follow him until he can be caught in the act.' Simmonds almost seemed annoyed at its simplicity.

'Yes, but you see, it isn't so easy. I never saw one of those men in my life.'

'What, you don't know what they look like?'

Pero shook his head:

'Nor does Hoffmann. Everything was through agents. I know nothing of their names. I have sent to many of those I used to know out there for information, but things have changed, I have received no answers.'

Pero roused himself, and unlocking the drawer of the writing-table took out a deed of agreement.

'Those are the three men,' he indicated the signatures, 'Cirilo Redoza, Bena Anouzin and Gabriel Edward Hicks. Redoza is a Spanish Jew, Anouzin an Armenian, and Hicks—'

'—is English?'

'Yes, I suppose so.'

'Well, it's something to know their nationalities. An Englishman, a Spanish Jew and an Armenian . . .'

'But I don't know another thing about them. We cannot trail every Spanish Jew, every Armenian we see—the Spanish Jew in San Rocco might pass as a San Roccan, the Armenian may be Americanized. And I believe this is a sort of revenge that an Englishman would not trouble himself with.'

'No, that's true,' Simmonds said suddenly, but nevertheless thought of the Carnation's lover. Hicks would be of the war generation—thirty-five at the least. The young man in the dressing-room had not looked that age—but it was just possible. Simmonds pulled up short: for him alone this case was impossible: it had spread now to include the Near East, the other side of the world. Scotland Yard, with its records, its routine, its official connection with the police of other countries, could in time trace those men. But Scotland Yard had no interest in crime in San Rocco, and San Rocco possessed only a semi-military gendarmerie. Simmonds wanted a holiday, he didn't want to comb the world. He should never have come, if Pero had been frank in the first place, he never would have come. He told this to Pero.

'I thought by the way you spoke you suspected someone you knew, someone from your household, even, or an employee. Mr Zaragoza, the best way is for me to resign. I'll hand you back your cheque and—'

Pero was on his feet:

'You can't! You have a contract, you have taken my money—'

'I'm giving it you back!' Simmonds felt in his pocket, but no dramatic gesture was to be allowed him. The money was sewed up in several compartments about his underclothing, as he had been taught to do by a canny mother when he first left home.

Suddenly Pero was all smiles, he patted Simmonds's shoulder:

'Perhaps you are right. Very well, I do not regret having enjoyed your company. Let us not quarrel, let us sleep, and in the morning we will see how much money it is fair and right for you to return.'

Simmonds regarded Pero suspiciously. There was something behind his eagerness to agree. However, he would say nothing more until morning. When he reached the exotic bedroom, with the chromium plated bedstead and the tinted sheets, almost indecent couch for an ex-superintendent, he congratulated himself on his decision to throw up the case. It had been some wild whim of Pero's to engage him, but it wouldn't work. No harm in keeping enough money to cover his expenses and the time he had lost . . . full of dollars the fair sandy head fell back on the lace-edged pillow. Simmonds slept.

Pero's cheerful 'Good morning' woke Simmonds to broad daylight, and to a continuation of the conversation of the evening before.

'I have been talking to Hoffmann,' Pero flitted round in his quaint pyjamas, 'he agrees with me: we have no legal hold over you. But when I picked on you, on an officer from the most famous detective force in the world, a man of the nation famed for the honourableness of its dealings, I thought I had found someone whom I could trust. And that is a great thing,' he smiled sadly, persuasively. 'In the world of men, and you like myself have knocked about in the world of men, it is the greatest thing.'

Simmonds glumly stroked his chin: he saw what was happening to him, but at this hour of the morning he had very little resistance.

'When I spoke to the Carnation on the telephone this morning,' Pero continued slyly, 'she could not believe that you had even hesitated. She is impressed by your courage and your will power.'

'Oh, is she.'

'But, my friend, you are quite right in one thing: the task is too complicated for one man. You must have help. My funds are unlimited, tell me how many assistants you require, name your own men—ten, twenty, fifty, tell me what you need. Place agents at the key points, at the harbour, at the railway station, order everything as you would in England.'

Pero broke off as Saco came in with coffee and delicately baked rolls. Simmonds wondered if the visit had been opportunely timed, and then, because he had wondered, realized that after all the case engaged his professional interest.

'Well,' he admitted, 'I did say I would stay here a month.

I don't mind doing that, but I can't promise you anything. Very likely I'll need some help, but I don't know who to get hold of. The trouble is, as a private person here, it's not going to be easy—seeing that I've got to work outside the home circle.'

Simmonds dipped his roll: Pero took one turn up and down the room and then faced him with decision:

'Mr Simmonds, you are perfectly right, you are always perfectly right. You require authority and an official position. That you shall have.' Pero almost ran to the door. 'Hoffmann! Hoffmann!'

The German appeared in elegant pyjamas, wearing steel spectacles on the end of his nose, and carrying a note-book.

'Hoffmann, order the car, put on formal dress, we are going to call on his Excellency.'

'Hi—what's his this—' Simmonds swung out of bed— 'what's his Excellency got to do with it?'

'But certainly!' Pero was very excited. 'He shall create you chief of the criminal investigation department of San Rocco. That is a thing which does not now exist. Don Miguel will do what I ask—you shall have his commission!'

## CHAPTER 7

### THE MINISTRY OF SANITATION

The palace of his Excellency Don Miguel de Valuque stretched along one side of the square with the fountains through which Simmonds had passed on his way from the docks. Wearing a dark tweed suit and a bowler hat Simmonds sat beside Pero, frock-coated, and opposite to Hoffmann, equally stiffened up and suffering phlegmatically some agonies from the little folding seat of Pero's limousine. The car swept past the lackadaisical sentries in the yellow uniforms of the Republican Guard to the not very imposing entrance. They waited for a short time in a broad and empty hall, into which drifted the sounds of a typewriter and a radio, and then they were beckoned along a corridor into an anteroom presided over by an officer in a bright yellow uniform, with a waxed moustache and a wasp waist.

In face of Pero's energy it was impossible to do anything but to be carried along: Simmonds was simply waiting for Don Miguel to squash the whole idea, and then he could withdraw, to England and to his holiday, with a good grace.

The waspy major went out and came back with a secretary, who treated Pero so obsequiously that Hoffmann, seeing Simmonds's stare, found time to whisper:

'Señor Zaragoza finances the entire Don Miguel ministry.'

Simmonds had not absorbed this interesting information before Don Miguel himself came forward to greet them, in the dim shuttered room more finely proportioned than the bad French furniture which filled it.

Don Miguel was delighted to see Pero, he hoped that the fire had not proved serious, he spoke about the dancing of some ladies at the hotel afterwards, and on being reminded that Simmonds was English, continued the gossip in a stilted hesitant English. Then it occurred to his Excellency that they might all sit down, and while he mildly listened, Pero explained the reason for the visit—these untoward events at the Acropolis, the necessity for not troubling the republican police, who were busy no doubt on more important matters —his Excellency smiled—and the desire of Pero to keep down all public expenditure.

'It is suggested, in fact, your Excellency, that this distinguished English police officer, one of the first of Scotland Yard, should be granted for a short period at least such official powers as will help him in solving this mystery.'

'Of course, my dear Zaragoza—why not?'

'Then you agree? You give a signed commission?'

'I will attend to the matter myself.'

Simmonds intercepted a warning look from Hoffmann to Pero. Pero nodded, and turned to Don Miguel:

'Is it possible for that to be done this afternoon?' Pero asked firmly.

'Yes, yes. Of course . . .' Don Miguel looked vaguely at his nails. 'Then there will be the question of expense . . .'

'Señor Simmonds will be paid by myself. As this matter does not require extra expenditure it need not go before the Chamber. And I had thought,' he added, 'of erecting a drinking fountain in the square, for the good of the citizens and commemorating the name of Don Miguel.'

His Excellency didn't seem to have grasped this last suggestion. He looked from one to the other:

'But why—if I may trouble you to tell me—cannot General Simmonds act without any special commission?'

Pero patiently explained it all over again, Don Miguel nodding agreement at all points. When Pero had finished the president rose and held out his hand. Pero ignored it, and hiding his exasperation asked if the matter could be arranged at once—immediately, before they left.

Don Miguel was evidently thinking out some polite excuse when a farther door opened and Carlotta came bouncing in.

'But, of course, Miguel,' she exclaimed, when Pero had outlined the situation, 'there is no difficulty at all. We shall have a criminal investigation department in San Rocco, modelled on the lines of Scotland Yard, and at no expense to the Treasury. Who can possibly object, except the crooks? And the crooked vote,' she beamed at Simmonds, 'is practically unimportant. Besides, Miguel has another four years to run. Now, let me see, you must have accommodation. There's the Ministry of Sanitation—that's empty. And their uniforms—all you have to do is to change the buttons!'

Simmonds achieved speech:

'Excuse me, sir and madam, I'm afraid I can't do that—I'm only here for a month, at Mr Zaragoza's personal request—'

'Oh, but you'll stay on afterwards and build up an organization for us!' Carlotta was already on her way to a desk, where she picked up a pen and began to write.

'I'm afraid that's impossible—' Simmonds began.

'I'm afraid it is,' echoed a tired voice from the background. Carlotta looked up sharply:

'And why is it impossible, Miguel?' she demanded.

'I don't think General Simmonds will be able to work very well with Colonel Sixola.'

'You are always afraid of Sixola!'

'Yes, but after all . . .'

'Colonel Sixola is the Chief of Police,' Hoffmann explained in an undertone while Carlotta eyed her husband fiercely. But suddenly she relaxed and, smiling, kissed her husband on the cheek.

'But, of course, you are not afraid of anyone. And Sixola can't say anything if we send Señor Simmonds to him for help and advice. They can work together—he'll have some ideas, perhaps,' she added, hopefully. 'Now,' she took Simmonds by the arm, 'everything will be all right. I'll see that the commission is sent along, and the authority to take over the Ministry of Sanitation. And we'll send an adjutant with you to introduce you to Colonel Sixola. I'm not going to keep you now, but when you have time you are going to have tea with me, and if everything doesn't go well you have only to come to me and I'll see that it's done.'

The headquarters of the Chief of Police, where a bewildered Simmonds found himself twenty minutes later, were in a wing of the Ministry of Justice: the soldiers on guard here were noticeably smarter than those outside the palace, and they were carrying genuine looking rifles instead of carbines. Even with the waspy major as cicerone it took much longer to get into the presence of Colonel Sixola than it had taken to reach Don Miguel. He was just putting down the telephone when the party was ushered in.

'Yes,' he said, when the waspy major had explained, 'her Excellency was speaking to me. And this—' he stared at Simmonds penetratingly— 'is the man?'

Sixola wore civilian clothes with a military bearing: he was short and squat and dynamic. When the major had concluded, Sixola looked at Simmonds with amused eyes.

'Naturally if it is the wish of his Excellency, and of Señor Zaragoza, I have nothing more to say. But for Señor Zaragoza's sake I hope it will turn out to be a mare's nest

—this sequence of mysterious accidents. I should have said, myself, that a new fire brigade would have been more to the point. Still, when you have traced the criminal, I shall be happy to congratulate you.'

That moment, when Sixola laughed at him, was for Simmonds a turning point. He had been saving up another resignation scene for Pero, to take place that afternoon, but now . . . well, it would be nice to show the sarcastic Sixola a thing or two . . .

Already, as they drove back to the Acropolis, Simmonds had begun to plan. There was the fire to investigate and—a thing he had forgotten—the Carnation and her chauffeur to interview, supposing her abduction was part of the same series. Then he must consider whether it was possible to write to a friend at the Yard, with a view to some unofficial help in tracing the three unknowns in Europe.

That afternoon, while the rest of San Rocco was asleep, Simmonds wrote down a list of things to be done in a small round hand on the back of an envelope. Detection, he knew, is hard work and nothing else. He had a pretty hopeless problem, but by taking one thing at a time, and sticking to it, he had a fair chance of success. San Rocco, after all, was not very large, and the criminal or criminals must be in San Rocco. He began to feel almost cheerful, particularly as he need do nothing but sit in Pero's over-comfortable arm-chair and think, nothing until the official warrant arrived. And, with any luck, that would not be for several days. But Simmonds was to be afforded no such excuse for delay: Pero and Hoffmann were still dozing when a messenger from the palace arrived with the document duly signed and sealed. Used to the dilatory officialdom of England, Simmonds stared at it in dismay. With it was enclosed a letter from Don Miguel, who, in his capacity of Field Marshal in Chief, granted Arthur Simmonds the temporary and honorary rank of captain. Enclosed also was the authority to take over certain offices.

Simmonds, having read and re-read the documents, consigned them to his breast pocket, gripped his bowler hat and set out—to clear his head, to think. And, of course, if he did happen to pass the Ministry of Sanitation there would be no harm in taking a look at it.

It was still very hot: no San Roccan had yet ventured out: Captain Simmonds, however, was used to wearing woollen underclothing in an English heat wave: but he would have agreed with anyone that it was hot.

Simmonds did happen to pass the Ministry of Sanitation —a dirty marble-faced building, once a private house but now overtaken by the spread of the dock and warehouse quarter. A small girl was fast asleep on the threshold of the door, which was open. Simmonds stepped over her and entered. The rooms on the ground floor were quite empty, plaster had flaked from the walls and the paint was blistered. Shallow stone stairs led to the next floor, which seemed in rather better repair. But if they thought that he was going to sit down upon a soap box in the middle of the floor and —but, hullo, this room looked more like it—there was a desk here, and a typewriter and—and a voice inquired in negligent English:

'Is there anything, within reason, that I can do for you just now?'

The speaker was a tall thin youth with golden hair, a receding chin and an expression of the utmost good-will. Bare to the waist, his trousers were hitched up with a club tie, and with the razor in one hand he indicated a tin basin:

'I'm just shaving, really. But don't mind me. You don't happen to have any soap, do you?'

Simmonds had a technique for meeting the unexpected: he stood still and said nothing.

It was clear that the youth without a chin was camping out in what had once been an office: a water melon and an open tin of milk stood on a filing cabinet: there was a spirit stove and a bubbling tin kettle in the formal marble fireplace, and a red plush sofa was obviously doing duty as a bed.

'I'm just going to make some tea. Please don't watch the kettle, there's a general idea that kettles don't like it. Perhaps you'll stop and have some. Some tea, I mean.'

'Tea!' Simmonds spoke at last.

'Tea,' corroborated the youth. 'I suppose,' he continued,

'you are ex-Superintendent Simmonds, and you have come to take over the ex-Ministry of Sanitation?'

'Well, how did you know that?'

'News travels fast here, comparatively. And you obviously do look like an ex-superintendent. And I—' he wiped his hands on a towel—'since we are being personal, am the ex-Minister of Sanitation. Aubrey Wilkinson.'

Simmonds found himself shaking hands.

'They gave up sanitation here,' continued the youth, diving into a shirt, 'six months ago. Not that they ever had it to give up. They gave up, to be precise, *trying* to have it. In the first flush of enthusiasm we—that's the Ministry—opened up all the drains. Unluckily no one knew how to close them, the vital statistics began to show a very strange curve, and the Ministry was axed. Do you have three lumps or two?'

'Three.'

'How I came to be the Minister is a long story. But then I'm English, and her Excellency has a great admiration for the English. I only should have given you two lumps, because this milk is sweetened. I hope you don't mind?'

Simmonds looked at him with a twinkle:

'Is this all true?'

Aubrey looked at him with the blankness of innocence:

'True? Does it sound strange? It's positively commonplace for San Rocco. The lousy thing is that somehow or other they forgot to pay me. Well, you know, Don Miguel is an ornament without power, and they're quite poor, and Carlotta's enthusiasm over-runs her discretion, and her purse. So I had, you see, to destrain on the premises, until something turned up, which in this case happens to be you. By the by—' his tone was earnest and friendly—'forgive me mentioning it, but I hope you took care of the financial end of things, so far as concerns yourself?'

'Well,' Simmonds said slowly, 'it happens that Mr Zaragoza's standing everything.'

'Then that's perfect! We shall be quite all right.'

'*We?*'

'Of course. If you take over the Ministry of Sanitation,

you take over me. And you know, really, I can help you quite a lot. I speak the San Roccan dialect, and I seem to have got to know something about the underworld here, which is going to be useful to you. And about the overworld too, I mean the political situation.'

Simmonds scratched his head.

'I don't know what you have in mind,' Aubrey ran on happily, 'and I suppose we shall have to begin slowly. There'll be some men to enrol, I think I can find the right fellows, and there'll be things like a fingerprint bureau, that would be useful, and luckily there's plenty of room here. We shall need some cells, perhaps, and a morgue and a dark-room, and an experimental laboratory, and a—'

'Hey, hey—' Simmonds's easy laughter cut short the catalogue. 'That's all very fine, but I'm not here to build up a ruddy Scotland Yard, whatever Carlotta may think. I'm here just for one thing, and if you want to help me you've got to forget all those fancy ideas.'

'As you say, Mr Simmonds. What do we do first, then?'

Simmonds made a show of looking at his watch:

'It wouldn't be a bad time to go and take a peep at the Acropolis theatre.'

Aubrey reached for his coat:

'All right, then, we'll go along, shall we?'


CHAPTER 8

THE MAN WITH THE BIG HEAD

News, as Aubrey had said, travelled fast in San Rocco, and as soon as they entered the theatre a curious crowd of stage-hands, cleaners and workmen collected and began to follow them round. Some said that Simmonds was after an international gang of jewel thieves, others that he represented a salvage company, others that he tracked a murderer. Still others, recognizing Aubrey, thought that a grand investigation of water-closets was in progress.

When at last they had shaken off the crowd they set to work to examine the gutted store-room. José the fireman had stoutly affirmed that nothing had been touched, that he or his deputy had been on guard every minute since the fire. Simmonds grunted, and poked about among the débris. Aubrey came up to his side:

'Mr Simmonds, shall I order two sieves?

'Sieves?'

'Don't we sieve all this, and find probably the trouser button of the fire-bug? We don't? No sieves? Perhaps you are right. However.' Cheerful under his disappointment Aubrey contented himself with observing sadly the heap of charred lace which had once decorated a can-can. Simmonds had turned his blue eye upwards.

'That ventilator, José, what happens the other side?'

'The other side, Captain? Number One dressing-room for the girls.'

'Is it empty now?'

'Yes, yes, they don't come yet for half an hour.'

Simmonds followed José to the dressing-room: the de luxe architecture of the auditorium had stopped short at the stage backing, and this was just like any other dressing-room. Simmonds stood on one of the wash-basins and observed the other side of the ventilator.

'Does it tell you anything?' inquired Aubrey.

'What does it tell *you*?'

'Me? I should say, first, that since the door was locked, the ventilator was the only way through which a combustible might have been introduced. Second, that it isn't really accessible without a step-ladder, and third, that it was closed at the time of the fire, otherwise the girls would have noticed the smoke before the old lady. Which means that unless the fire started of its own sweet will, some delayed action-fuse was introduced previously.'

Simmonds poked at the ventilator with a pencil.

'Hm. You can open and close it from this side. So that some burning cloth, or something, could be thrown through from here, and the ventilator closed afterwards.'

'How about the girls?' Aubrey objected. 'The room would be pretty full of them, and unless it was a revolt of the chorus, and they were all in it, I don't see how it could be done.'

Simmonds descended from the wash-basin.

'If the girls were on the stage,' he argued patiently, 'they wouldn't be here, would they?'

'That seems perfectly logical. The only thing to do is to ask the girls if, when they were on the stage, they saw any unauthorized person in here. That's it, isn't it?'

'Now, just what do you mean?' Simmonds regarded the youth suspiciously.

'Only that the girls ought to be questioned, you know.'

'Ah.' Simmonds did not sound enthusiastic.

'Don't think,' Aubrey hastened to say, 'that the questioning of chorus girls interests me. However.'

'Oh, question them if you like. You can question every blooming person who was in the theatre last night, you can question the whole of San Rocco. But personally I'm not a complete police force rolled into one.'

'Naturally not,' Aubrey conceded, as a babble of voices, Spanish, French, German, English and American, indicated that the girls were beginning to arrive for the evening performance. 'But all the same, I don't think it would be a bad thing if I was to grill the birds a little, what do you say?'

'All right, then.'

Simmonds was not sorry to get rid of Aubrey; he wanted to check up on the fire exit which had been mysteriously open on the night of the fire. 'Billy' had used it, no doubt, but then so might have the fire-bug. But adventuring in the upper storey corridors he could find no way from the Carnation's dressing-room, or the fire-exit, to the wardrobe store-room that wouldn't be, during a performance, under the eye of one or the other of the theatre officials—the fireman, or the stage-doorkeeper. Any unauthorized person using the fire exit as a means of access to the store-room would have been seen. Aubrey's voice interrupted him:

'Mr Simmonds, please come and see what I've got for you.'

Looking over the rail he saw Aubrey below, with one of the birds he had promised to grill—a plump blonde in one of those sailor suits which make young girls look either four or forty. Simmonds descended with a now-then-what-is-all-this expression.

'This young woman has come comparatively clean,' announced Aubrey, pulling her forward. 'Now then, fraulein, sprechen sie alles to the captain. Tell him was sie mir haben spoken.'

The blonde faced Simmonds with an honesty that was transparent, and with the earnestness of her race.

'I have told,' she said dutifully, 'that on the night when the fire happened I was not working, and I came to the dressing-room and saw a girl who was with a man. So I went out of that room, and then in a little was the fire.'

'Go on, Trude,' Aubrey gently nudged her, 'who was this man?'

'The valet of Señor Zaragoza.'

'Known,' supplied Aubrey, 'as Saco. And the girl's name is Emilienne, but she isn't here yet, at the moment.'

'Oh.' Simmonds was not surprised to hear something against Saco, but he didn't allow the idea to run away with him.

That was all the girl had to say, and she wanted to get on with her make-up. Simmonds let her go.

'Pretty decent, do you think?'

'What—the girl?'

'No, no,' Aubrey deprecated, 'the clue.'

'I don't know. Saco's too young to be one of the unknowns. But he might be a tool, or a spy. That's possible.'

'And what sort of things happen up there?' Aubrey pointed upwards. Simmonds hesitated, and then decided to tell Aubrey about the Carnation and the Englishman 'Billy'.

'Lucky fellow,' said Aubrey. 'Or, perhaps, considering Pinks, not.'

'Pinks?'

'Vulgar for the Carnation. As regards her, the instructions are "handle with care".'

'I found her not a bad sort.'

Aubrey regarded Simmonds momentarily with a smile that awarded him the medal for simplicity. Then he continued:

'The Englishman would be Billy Wykes. He is the engineer in charge of the Grand Central Railway. The rail head is about eighty miles away, and he lives there and doesn't come into San Rocco. They're having some trouble with territorial rights.'

'And what do you know about him?'

'Very little. I should say he was Malvern and Emmanuel, Cambridge—or Pembroke, perhaps. No, I should think he just missed that, unless he had a couple of years there after the war. Which is all sheer deduction, from having seen him drink a cocktail once in a sort of a little bar.'

'Ah. Well, I'd like to have a chat with Mr Wykes some time. And now,' Simmonds glanced at his watch, 'what about this girl Emilienne?'

'I'll go and see. You go into Calcagno's office or some place, and I'll bring her there.'

Calcagno was not in his office, and Simmonds took the liberty of sitting in his chair. Of course, there was Calcagno himself to consider: age and type fitted. But then he was holding down too good a job. There was as yet no limitation to the suspects: but he was earning his pay, and there was nothing for it but a determined attack on patient and traditional lines.

Aubrey arrived with the girl Emilienne, who had been induced to come along on false pretences, thinking that the manager had sent for her. She wasn't inclined at first to answer questions.

'Now, mademoiselle,' Aubrey encouraged, 'it will be more convenient for you to answer the questions of the captain here, than to wait for the Chief of Police to ask you the same ones. The prisons in San Rocco are very bad: regarding the sanitation I can speak for myself.'

The girl drew closer her shabby silk wrap stained with lipstick and looked from one to the other distrustfully.

'That's right, miss,' Simmonds was kind, 'there's nothing to worry about. We know you're a friend of Mr Saco, and that you were with him in the dressing-room when the others were on the stage. Now, why were you there?'

'Because I had hurt my ankle.'

In proof of which she presented an ankle which, anyhow, was bandaged under the thin stocking.

'And Mr Saco happened to hear that you were there, and came to see you?'

'He is a friend of mine.'

'Oh, yes, so we gathered.' Simmonds was heavily jovial. 'Now, was there any time when Mr Saco was alone in the dressing-room? Were you there all the time?'

'Yes. Yes, I am certain. My ankle was paining, and I did not like to walk.'

'And when did Mr Saco go?'

'Not till we heard there was a fire.'

'I see. And how long have you known Mr Saco?'

'About—about a week.'

Aubrey and Simmonds looked at each other. Saco might have been using the girl as an excuse for visiting the theatre, but the girl's evidence was probably truthful: and that ruled out the ventilator as a solution.

'All right,' Simmonds nodded towards the door. 'You can go for the moment.'

She stopped, hesitating in the doorway:

'You are looking for someone who might have started the fire, that is it, isn't it?'

'That's generally the idea,' Aubrey assured her, taking her fingers from the door-knob and closing the door and leading her back to her chair. 'And now tell us exactly what you know about that!'

She laughed in his face.

'You are very quick, mister. I don't know, it may be nothing, but I have seen a man in the corridor outside the wardrobe several times, when I have been waiting for my friend. This man was in rough clothes, like a workman, only

I know he wasn't one of the carpenters, and if he was, he has no reason to be in that place.'

'A San Roccan?'

'I imagine so. He was not very tall, and he had a very big head with thick black hair. He didn't like being seen, and when I looked at him he immediately began to walk like a man who is pretending that he is unoccupied.'

## CHAPTER 9

### SIMMONDS SMELLS A RAT

The girl Emilienne could give no more detailed description of the stranger: but one very important fact emerged from her evidence: she had last seen the man with the big head on the occasion, two days before the fire, when the store-room had been open for some hours for the return of a set of costumes which would not be needed owing to a change in the programme.

'What now?' inquired Aubrey, when the girl had been dismissed.

'We go back to the store-room. In a civilized country this would be a job for salvage experts, but we'll have to see what we can do.'

'It looks a pretty hopeless mess, on the whole,' Aubrey sighed when they had regained the gutted room. 'So far as I can see, the fire started over there—' he pointed to a corner where even the metal shelves were twisted—'and it looks as if a delayed action fuse, or anything of that sort, would have been completely demolished.'

'It's not very important,' Simmonds grunted, pushing back his bowler hat and glumly staring round. 'It wouldn't tell us much more than we already know, even if we did find something.'

Aubrey lit a cigarette:

'A little more ash won't hurt any one. Now *that* was a pretty costume!' He held up admiringly a confection of glass beads and copper foil. Then suddenly he dropped it and dived down into the pile from which he had taken it. Simmonds turned at his exclamation.

'What have you got?'

'The body!'

'What?'

Aubrey held up by its tail a large grey rat:

'Exhibit Number One. A dead rat.'

'You can keep it.' Simmonds was not in spirits. But then it occurred to him that even a rat should have a post-mortem, and he gingerly took hold of it.

'Well, now that's funny.'

'What's funny?' Aubrey inquired.

'This rat. It's not burned. Not even singed.'

'It was suffocated, perhaps. Those costumes where I found it aren't singed, anyway.'

'Where does all this sticky stuff come from?' Simmonds demanded suddenly, drawing his finger along the rat's back and then holding it to the light. 'Golden syrup, or something.'

'The stuff out of the fire extinguishers?'

'No, it's not that. It's—' Simmonds gave a low whistle —'it's more like glycerine. And if it's glycerine, my boy, then I bet I know how the fire was started!'

Aubrey waited patiently while Simmonds made another examination of the rat, rubbing the sticky substance between his finger-tips, and finally tasting it with the tip of his tongue.

'It was used in a shipping case, I remember, once,' Simmonds continued. 'Glycerine and something else—what was it? You ought to know, it's something that's used for drains . . .'

'Drains? Drains?' Aubrey threw himself into the position of thinking.

'Yes—a disinfectant. I shall get it in a moment—I know, permanganate of potash!'

'That is used for drains. But what exactly . . .'

'That's it!' Simmonds had been re-testing his memory. 'Glycerine and permanganate of potash, it was. As soon as they come in contact, they take fire spontaneously. They're not the only things, of course, that do that, but they can both of them be bought for toilet use, without rousing suspicion.'

'Well then, what do we look for? Permanganate of potash?'

'I don't think it's much good looking.' Simmonds was still cherishing the rat. 'There'd be some sort of a time bomb, containing the two substances, and that would be the first thing destroyed. Only this little beggar nosed round, probably upset the apple-cart, and burrowed in under those costumes, as far away from the fire as possible. But it must have been too hot for him after all, and he suffocated.'

'Well,' Aubrey hardly knew what to say, 'it's a handsome deduction.'

'You've got to account for the glycerine,' Simmonds maintained stoutly, 'if it is glycerine. We'll have to have that proved. And in the meantime—do you want a job?'

'What job?'

'Working round the chemists' shops, and finding out what purchases of glycerine and permanganate of potash have been made within the last few weeks.'

'Well, I can try. Only it's a pity we can't wait till the cool season.'

'There can't be very many chemists in San Rocco,' Simmonds insisted mildly. 'Now, if it was in London it would be a different matter. You don't stand a bad chance, and I thought you wanted to help me?'

Aubrey wrestled with disappointment: finally he held out his hand:

'All right. I'll do my best. Give me the rat.'

Simmonds handed it over:

'You can make a beginning in the morning. I've got a little call to make of my own.'

Simmonds's little call was to the villa of the Carnation, and thither he set out in a hired car while the morning was still bright and early. He had slipped away without telling Pero of his errand. Pero was fully absorbed in his daily business, and on the previous night Simmonds hadn't even seen him.

The hard automobile road ended abruptly three miles from the limits of the town, and was continued into the forest by a narrow road of red beaten earth. The big timber had mostly been cut, but undergrowth had sprung up on all sides hiding from each other a few scattered farms and small plantations. Half an hour of inferior going brought Simmonds to a newly painted direction post, and he turned down another red earth track which twisted for five or ten minutes, till the view suddenly opened, and across an unfenced clearing neatly planted with various crops, lay a long low white house with many red-roofed outbuildings and shady verandahs. A hundred yards from the house the track broadened out into a wide gravel sweep, running up to a dazzling terrace of white concrete, shaded with palms and roses and littered with gay umbrellas which threw mauve shadows over canvas chairs, shallow steps and earthenware jars spilling brilliant flowers. Simmonds dismounted, and a white-jacketed servant led him into a room that was black with shadow in spite of white plastered walls and the skin of a polar bear. The servant took off a card which said in printed script: *Mr Arthur Simmonds, Barons Court, W.* An aristocratic dog came by, looked at Simmonds, scratched, and went out. The servant returned.

'The señorita asks if you will please join her in the swimming pool.'

Simmonds, holding his bowler hat, measured his paces behind the servant's, and followed to a court at the other side of the house, where the reflection of white walls shivered in a turquoise pool. At that moment the Carnation, perhaps not having seen his arrival, took off from the diving-board. Glistening face and shoulders emerged at the other end of the bath, at Simmonds' toes.

'Ea! It's you!'

'Didn't the servant tell you?' Simmonds inquired suspiciously, closing his fingers over the dripping hand she offered him.

'Oh, he said there was a visitor, who looked—' she rolled

out of the water and over the edge of the bath—'very hot. And you do! Would you like to swim?'

'No, thank you. Not just now.'

'I think I could find a costume to fit.' She estimated his figure with sparkling eyes. And then suddenly standing up asked with a change of tone: 'Did you ask Pero what happened in Prinkipo?'

'Yes, thank you. It was in a theatre called the Prinkipo —not in the island of that name.'

'What does it matter?' She led the way to a group of chairs, and sitting down crossed the legs which the papers said had been insured for ten thousand pounds. 'I really didn't know much—Pero started to confide one day and then closed up. But I thought *you* ought to know.'

'Yes. Thank you.'

There was silence for a moment, while the water dripped from her brown limbs and was eaten up by the sun.

'I hear,' she said encouragingly, 'that you've been officially recognized?'

'Yes.'

'So that when you ask me questions, you can put me in prison if I don't answer them?'

Her look was mocking: she expected questions, then.

'Well, hardly that.' Simmonds was jocular. 'You wouldn't have any reason for not answering questions. And you want to find out who played that trick on you, don't you? I mean, when you were late for the gala performance?'

'Oh, that! Yes, of course.'

'And naturally you're anxious for Mr Zaragoza?'

'Oh, for Pero—yes. But sometimes I'm rather amused to see him in concern. The little Cæsar is then as excited as a woman.'

Thoughts floated to the surface in Simmonds's brain. The whole affair might be a childish prank on her part to scare her fat protector, cunningly based on his known fear of certain events in the past. He had had the details of the abduction from Hoffmann: there had been no witness except the Carnation herself. It might be some plan of hers to make Pero give up his San Roccan venture, for reasons, or for no reason but a whim. If the Carnation and Pero had a differ-ence of opinion, there was no telling what might result.

'You think a great deal more than you speak, Mr Sim-monds?'

Simmonds completed his thoughts, and then turned to her sagaciously:

'I was wondering if you would answer a certain question.'

'I told you there would be questions. What is it?'

'On the night of the fire,' Simmonds began, 'one of the emergency exits was found open. Now the funny thing about it was this: it had been opened by someone inside, and it had been kept open with a bit of wood. I wanted to ask you if you'd noticed it.'

'No, I didn't.' She shook her head. 'I never go along that passage.'

'Ah, you know which exit I mean!' It was the old tech-nique, but as good as any. The Carnation burst out laughing.

'I have walked into the little trap! And I always knew that it was you who was in my bathroom that night.'

'You've guessed right.'

'Oh, but it wasn't a guess. There was powder spilt on the floor, and someone in rubber heels had walked across it. I don't wear rubber heels.'

'And "Billy" doesn't either?'

She looked at him reproachfully:

'Billy hasn't rubber heels. It's perfectly true, I did open the emergency door for him, but these are things that hardly concern you.'

Simmonds wasn't upset by that first note of hostility. He apologized easily, and with a man-of-the-world attitude promised discretion on his part. If the door had been opened for a friend of hers, that settled that. He wasn't surprised, however, when she volunteered an explanation.

'Pero doesn't know about my friend, I needn't tell you that. I knew him before I knew Pero, once when he was making a railway in Mexico. And then, when Pero was in Europe, he was appointed to take over here.'

'And Pero wouldn't like it if he knew?'

'Oh, well, the engineer is in love, and he cannot hide it:

it's better for them not to meet. Pero has done a great deal for me,' she added simply. 'I can't forget that.'

Simmonds was inclined to give the Carnation some marks for sincerity: her exact relationship to Pero was puzzling: she obviously had an affection for him, and he obviously thought the world of her. But as an artist only? Perhaps it was that her first excitement and gratitude at being 'discovered' were now wearing thin, but fear or policy or consideration for Pero's feelings prompted her to keep the lover a secret. As if she had said all she intended to say on that subject, the Carnation now rose abruptly.

'I'll send for Enrique. He's been a little strange since he was knocked out, and I haven't let him drive my car again yet.' Stepping into the house, she called for the chauffeur, and a stiff, serious-faced young man in a white cotton jacket came hurrying. At the Carnation's order he recited all that had happened. He had been polishing the car outside the garage, in haste because his mistress must be punctual at the theatre, when suddenly he had heard a step behind him. 'I am just ready,' he had called out, thinking that it was the house-boy, when the blow had descended. He remembered nothing more until he woke up to find the Señorita bathing his head. He had been found huddled up against the wall at the back of the garage, so he had been told. Simmonds had seen the garage as he drove up. Some yards from the house, it was not far from the edge of the forest, which was only separated by a simple wire fence from the demesne. An assailant could easily have approached unnoticed.

'So you never even saw who it was?'

'No, señor.'

'Just before that time, did you ever see any strangers near the place?'

'No, señor. No one ever comes here.'

'But the servants—the men who work in the fields—are there any new ones, strange ones?'

'No, señor. They, like myself, all worked for the old master, before the Señorita came here.'

'Have you ever seen a dark, short man, with a lot of black hair, and a big head?'

'No,' Enrique shook his head, distressed at not being able to satisfy the señor. But there was a sudden exclamation from the Carnation:

'A short man, with a big head and dark hair—but that was the man who took Enrique's place—he was like that!'


# CHAPTER 10

## TWENTY-FIVE SANITARY INSPECTORS

The case was opening out nicely, Simmonds thought, and it was in a mood of optimism that he sought out Aubrey at headquarters. Something seemed to be up, when he arrived there, for the doorway was blocked with a crowd of men, women and children, and when he shouldered his way through he found on either side of the stairs a queue of the riff-raff of San Rocco.

'What's all this? Has anything happened?' he demanded of the man nearest to him. At the sound of his voice a ripple of excitement passed along the line—a score of cheerfully evil faces were turned towards him.

'Well, what is it?'

'Captain—' a swarthy hand clutched at his sleeve—'I am the father of ten children and I support two aunts and a female relative—'

'He is a liar!' Another had gripped Simmonds imploringly by the coat lapel. 'It is his aunts that support him. Now I, I do not talk about my family, but I say that I know many murderers . . .'

'Captain!'

'Captain, I was in the police force but by error I arrested a thief who had paid for his protection and I was wrongfully dismissed.'

'Captain, listen to no one except me—'

'Captain!'

From every side Simmonds was besieged, and it was only by sheer force that, ignoring their importunities, he reached the door of the main office. He slammed it shut and set his back against it, but the office was full of men too, the babble of voices and the stench of garlic. Above the clamour rose a voice, Aubrey's voice:

'That's all. I've got all your names now. Wait downstairs now for orders. Ah—' he had seen Simmonds—'Captain Simmonds, I've just been enrolling the first contingent. Now then—' he broke off to hustle the men out of the room. 'Clear out now, please, and be silent, or you will be dismissed instantly, and even quicker than that.'

It took Aubrey some little time to hustle them out, and when the room was clear at last and he had locked the door, unaware apparently of Simmonds's dangerously resigned silence he drifted cheerfully over to the desk, where he blotted the last page in a handsome looking ledger and rattled on with an air of work well done:

'The thing they want more than anything else is discipline. That wouldn't be so difficult if we could put them in uniform, but we haven't any uniforms, and they're plain-clothes men anyway. I've been wondering whether we ought to buy some stars—you can get some very good-looking tinsel stars in a shop near the cathedral. They're for decorating the saints, and I suppose that might be considered sacrilege, and we mustn't get the church against us. But we shall have to fake up some sort of badge, don't you think. It makes all the difference to a man to have something he might lose if he doesn't behave himself. Like cutting away epaulets in the army. They're always cutting them away in the San Roccan army, most impressive, and in questions of discipline it's always best to follow the customs of the country.'

'So those gentlemen,' Simmonds picked his words, 'have been enrolled by you as plain-clothes detectives?'

'Exactly!' Aubrey swung himself on to the edge of the desk and negligently lit a cigarette. 'Twenty-five to start with. And there's a whole body of hangers-on we can recruit from if we need them, more or less.'

'And what, Mr Wilkinson, are you going to do with them?'

'That I want to discuss with you. But I have some ideas, naturally.'

'You have, have you?'

'Ah, well,' Aubrey was modest but unabashed, 'I rather seem to get ideas, particularly when I've been lying fallow. I won't always have ideas, I'm afraid— there're some ways in which I am exceptionally lazy. But I haven't been doing a great deal lately, and I'm due for one of my periodic bursts of energy. That's just my way of living—a sort of hibernation, followed by a renaissance, a wonder year, a cinquecento. Then, inevitably—' he waved a deprecatory hand—'the energy is used up, I get tired, disillusioned, thought passes from the rococo to the debased. Then I simply have to wait for the next cycle. However, I don't want to talk about myself. I'll tell you what I had in mind: I've made some notes—ah, yes, here we are.'

Simmonds was wondering if Aubrey was really mad or only seemed so. Or drunk.

'Now—' Aubrey straightened out his notes. 'First of all, I thought, we need some men to comb the chemists' shops. I've made out a list, and with five of the men on the job we can cover the whole island in a few days. They can ask questions without arousing suspicion, and that's a thing we couldn't do. Now, for the others, we'll need a certain number on duty here for whatever else turns up, and the rest I thought we ought to sprinkle about the Acropolis—we'll get them taken on as porters, night-watchmen, commission-aires, and so forth. That's something the uniformed branch ought to see to, but the police seem to be busy preparing for a political coup d'état, don't you think? and Pero really ought to have more protection. That's really preventing crime, rather than detecting it, I suppose, but there's always the chance of catching 'em red-handed. Not so good as detection, but it's results that matter, I suppose. Or isn't it? Are you a purist?'

Simmonds had been letting Aubrey go on talking, but Aubrey really seemed to want to know if Simmonds was a purist, and Simmonds had time to collect his wits and inquire:

'And who's going to pay for all this? Saratoga *may*, but wouldn't it have been just as well to consult him first?'

'Oh, it won't cost the old trunk a dollar.'

'Then who's footing the bill?'

'Actually, the taxpayers of San Rocco. I've fixed it all up with Carlotta. She sent for me this morning, to see how things were going on, and we got talking as it is so conveniently expressed, and we found out that the Ministry of Sanitation was still being milked by someone at the Treasury. Yes, I know, I told you it had been axed, but the Treasury hadn't ever been notified, and the matter won't come up till the audit at the end of the year. In the meantime there'd been a spot of peculation going on. Well, I didn't see why we shouldn't peculate too. There's nothing to stop us drawing any amount up to the limit of the original grant. With luck, I shall get my back salary, and when we want anything, we've only got to send in a chit for a thousand drain-pipes, or a couple of man-hole covers.'

'And what do we want with a couple of man-hole covers?'

Aubrey wasn't sure whether Simmonds was being dense by nature or on purpose.

'We don't want a couple of man-hole covers, but we could do with, say, a staff car. Now, supposing that costs five hundred dollars—well, all we have to do is to send in a chit for a thousand drain-pipes at half a dollar a-piece. I've put down our plain-clothes men as sanitary inspectors, twenty-five of them, and I have, as a matter of fact, ordered a car. Then there's a couple of rotary brushes—that covers a microphoto apparatus, and—' Aubrey broke off as the telephone buzzed. 'Excuse me.'

Simmonds was wondering how soon there was a boat back to England.

'That rat—' Aubrey turned from the telephone excitedly. 'The analytical report has just come through.' He turned back to the 'phone. 'Yes, yes, it's the Criminal Investigation Department speaking.'

Simmonds did want to hear about the rat.

'Yes, yes . . .' Aubrey, at the telephone, repeated the

news. 'You're sure? Toilet glycerine of a very pure brand? That's excellent!'

Simmonds was looking almost alert and interested as Aubrey finally hung up.

'I got the chief analyst at the laboratory attached to the Agricultural School to confirm your brilliant suggestion. Put it down as a sample of sewage, but the rat won't have to mind that. I say—that's a good thing to know, isn't it? Now, what was I going to ask you—ah, I know—the finger-print system. I—'

Simmonds planted himself truculently in front of Aubrey:

'Now look here, young man, this may be your wonder year, but it isn't mine. I didn't come here to run a criminal investigation department, and I'm not going to.'

Aubrey was surprised:

'But didn't you want to know about the rat?'

'Well—there's no harm in that, I dare say.'

'And didn't you tell me to check up on the chemists' shops? Then, Mr Simmonds, what's wrong? Now,' he continued quickly, without giving Simmonds time to answer, 'about these finger-prints.'

The telephone was busy again. Simmonds sat down and took a deep breath.

'Ah, yes, Doctor Falzego . . . yes, yes. That was correct. Oh, naturally . . . Who was that? . . . He did? . . . Then we'll get in touch with you . . . certainly . . . no, no . . . not at all . . . yes, yes . . . Certainly, then. Goodbye.' Aubrey turned from the telephone. 'That's Dr Falzego, he's one of the best surgeons. I've arranged for him to be attached to our staff on the chance we may need him.'

'A surgeon?' Simmonds inquired with mild innocence.

'Yes.'

'Then he couldn't tackle a mental case?'

'I don't know, but we could get in touch with a mental expert too.' His hand strayed towards the telephone. 'A good idea. A psychologist, you mean?'

'No, I don't.' Simmonds grabbed the telephone. 'And what other little plans have you got up your sleeve?'

'I'll tell you. We ought to have a press contact bureau—

that's myself, for the moment. Then evening classes for the men: you can lecture. Then—'

'*Then* we take over the army, navy, and the air force?' Simmonds inquired heavily. Aubrey began to realize that Simmonds wasn't being enthusiastic. Simmonds slammed on his bowler hat and walked out of the door. Four sanitary inspectors were playing cards on the top step.

'Oh, go on playing, don't mind me, don't mind me,' Simmonds said blandly, but checked as the telephone sounded a third time. He would perhaps just see what else the lunatic had been up to. It would make a good story. The office door was thrown open:

'Ah!' Aubrey was delighted to see that he had not gone. 'Captain Simmonds, it's Colonel Sixola. He wants to speak to you.'

Now, as Simmonds had already mentally resigned from his position there was no necessity for him to speak to the chief of police, whose semi-official subordinate he was, and he did indeed hesitate. But the four sanitary inspectors were looking at him, and Aubrey was holding open the door, and the telephone receiver was lying on the table. Simmonds went back.

'Captain Simmonds? This is Sixola. You are very well?'

Simmonds grunted.

'Excellent. And have you the time, and would you have the great courtesy to come to my office for a little conference?'

Simmonds considered that he might as well go and tell Sixola that he had resigned and was leaving the island by the next boat. It would be a courtesy to tip him off as regards the discoveries already made. He told Sixola that he was on the way.

Other sanitary inspectors were having their dinner at the foot of the stairs, and outside the open door a big grey touring car was drawn up. Upon seeing Simmonds, a handsome-looking youth in a singlet and white trousers jumped up from the running-board and threw open the door with an inviting smile. The San Roccan sun contributed to the invitation, and Simmonds grandly stepped into the car, which was represented in the Treasury accounts by a thousand drain-pipes.

The powerful, ungainly car almost filled the narrow street, but the driver did not on that account sacrifice speed. With one hand on the horn, he used the other to swing the car from corner to corner, under arches, up streets that were almost staircases and through alleys that were almost tunnels. Then, after a final burst of speed across the great square, the car was brought to its haunches in front of the police headquarters. Simmonds, noticing once more the efficient-looking gendarmes on guard, remembered what Aubrey had said about a political coup d'état, but, preparing the attitude he would adopt towards Sixola, he did not concern himself with that.

Sixola was in uniform for this occasion. He received Simmonds with a false and genial smile. In the big, empty office his desk was dramatically placed. Simmonds knew himself the technique of interviews and recognized that the chair to which he was waved was in a position which had been subtly calculated. Sixola's opening chatter was a mere cover for the skirmish of their personalities. Sixola's brown, quick eye played over Simmonds, whose little blue eyes, bloodshot, and underhung with pouches, took in Sixola. When Sixola asked how Simmonds was getting on, the phrasing of the question suggested that, of course, he hadn't got on at all. Simmonds, in answering, was aware that he was being pumped, but he had to give himself the little triumph of telling Sixola that he had already secured an accurate description of one of the men concerned, and that he had proved to his own satisfaction how the fire had been started.

'My congratulations,' said Sixola genially. 'At one end of affairs you have made a great deal of progress. But there is, of course, the other end.'

'I've been thinking about that too.'

'It's the obvious line of approach.' Sixola smiled. 'It's occurred to me, Captain, that I might be able to help you. Inquiries abroad under my signature might carry more weight. I've been able to help the police of other countries in the past, and now they should be willing to help me—to help us.'

'I'd only be too glad.' Simmonds could be affable too. 'The less routine work I have to do, the better.'

'Then will you leave it to me to request information regarding these three persons of whom Señor Zaragoza knows so strangely only the names?'

'With pleasure.' Simmonds recognized the professional jealousy that had stimulated Sixola's offer.

'Then that's agreed.' Sixola played with an ivory ruler. 'There was one other thing I wanted to mention . . .'

Simmonds sat and waited for it.

'I hope you will not misunderstand me,' Sixola continued, 'but you know, innovations are not very popular in San Rocco. Already in certain quarters I have heard criticism of the idea of a criminal investigation department.'

Simmonds opened his mouth to speak.

'No, no—' Sixola held up his hand. 'I know what you are going to say. That you are only concerned with one crime. That is true. Personally, I should welcome the formation of a detective force, but we can hardly expect the criminals who unfortunately exist, even in San Rocco, to agree?'

'I didn't expect them to.'

'And,' continued Sixola, 'I fear that as a foreigner you may meet with resistance. There are many here who resent the presence of foreigners in important positions in the island. There are many who would rather be poor and free and happy than be civilized as highly as, say, the United States.'

'I can understand that.' Simmonds could see the hint. Strange, but he hadn't yet told Sixola that he was resigning. Sixola's next sentence, however, put an end to any thoughts of that.

'So, Captain Simmonds, I must warn you to take good care of yourself. You run very grave risks. If you felt, under the circumstances, that you should not be called upon to face them, everyone would understand. You've been rather rushed into a false position, I think?'

'No,' Simmonds answered slowly, 'I've engaged to do a

certain thing. It's not working out quite as I imagined, but that's no reason for backing out, is it?'

'Then you are really going through with it?'

'Yes!'


# CHAPTER 11

## THE THOUSAND CUTS

In the seventh year of Ernestine Foster's Hollywood stardom things began to go wrong, the English-Danish-Italian actress with the golden hair and the black eyes—hair that was golden by nature and not by art—wearied of the stories that had been served out to her. Every film in which she starred was a financial loss, and on each next film was money lavished and a comeback promised. Only when the coffers were empty did the executives understand that for seven years she had been offering them advice: Hollywood had found every rôle for her but one similar to that which had brought her sudden world fame in the great days of the continental silent film.

'The Foster is right!' They all cried out, with one voice, and a dozen writers set to work to copy that first and classic film. But it had been left too late, a purity campaign was on the horizon and now the big clouds heavy with the soft white snow of artless innocence broke over the studios, the gunmen's molls of yesterday became governesses, and children romped in a world where everything was clean and kind. Ernestine Foster was left out.

The Foster, however, had lived frugally during the years of her success, and she was very rich. After six months' work on a story, aided by a young author who was too dazzled by her personality to resist even her wildest ideas, she collected together the director, the cameraman and even some of the cast of that first classic film. All her money was poured into the production, the money of the director and the sweat of the author, who had no money. For a year the film was made and remade, shot and reshot. Ernestine Foster acted her head off, five hundred thousand feet of film was exposed, her leading man walked out, the film ceased to be news and became a legend. Then she decided to remake it in colour. Six months passed, and at last there was something that could be called a film: the first copy was twenty thousand feet. Desperate cutting reduced it to fifteen thousand before Ernestine sacked the cutter, replaced a thousand feet, and refused to allow another inch to be removed. Although unsuitable for ordinary commercial entertainment distributing companies began to bargain for the right to handle it. Critics privileged to see the film agreed that the plot was obscure, and where not obscure, then incredible: that The Foster, unchecked by her fond and out-moded director, had overacted to the point of the ridiculous. But on the other hand there was the enormous publicity which it had received, the fact that it was one of the first full-length dramas to be taken entirely in colour, there was the beauty of the star, whose gold hair, black eyes and peachy skin had been exploited against every possible background, and there was honest admiration for her reckless challenge to the purity campaigners. On these points Ernestine was able to sell a half-share in the film at a price which enabled her to pay everyone, except the young author, but left her penniless. Her troubles, however, had only begun. The censors, both in England and America, demanded hundreds of cuts and refused to pass the title, which was *Leda*. The theory seemed to be that the story was impossible to understand, but that if understood it would corrupt the morals of old and young. The story was, indeed, unseemly, and, worse, the vicious protagonist was the heroine herself, unrepentant and finally triumphant. There followed six months of negotiation and of law-suits. At the end of that time Ernestine, poor but proud, refused to allow the resultant travesty to be exhibited. Litigation followed, Ernestine won her case, and the film passed back into her own control. But no one could see it, no one dared handle it—no one except Pero. He sought an interview with the now almost demented actress, and offered to show *Leda* in San Rocco, where there was no censorship. Ernestine, almost mad for self-exhibition, threw her arms round his neck and gave him, free of charge, a copy of the film. Pero arranged for a personal appearance of the star and chartered a special boat to bring to San Rocco at his own expense a dozen important executives and a score of newspapermen. This would be terrific publicity for him and for San Rocco: in all the world only in San Rocco could the masterpiece be seen, only San Rocco was sufficiently enlightened, sufficiently cultured. He also hoped to draw the attention of the film world to the sunny climate and the variegated scenery of the island. Who knew? perhaps it would become a second Hollywood—and all the suitable land was owned by Pero. Everything had been prepared, when the young author, now not so young, woke to the fact that the presentation of *Leda* would be his ruin. He found an overlooked clause in his contract, and brought an injunction. Ernestine Foster succumbed to a nervous breakdown and died in a sanatorium. Pero appealed against the injunction, and won his case. But the moment has passed, the film was already old-fashioned, and America was occupied with its depression. Pero waited his time: Hollywood was sick, producers began to consider a change of air. Pero announced the world première of Ernestine Foster's *Leda*. This was ten days after Simmonds had established himself on the island. In part it was preparation for this event that had absorbed Pero's attention, and though plans had been modified, the exhibition of the film was still an important event.

Simmonds, disgruntled but turned from resigning by Sixola's professional jealousy, had devoted himself for a couple of days to the routine work of following up existing clues. Aubrey had been full of helpful ideas which had come to nothing, and, incorrigibly fertile, had been doing Simmonds didn't know what with the organization at headquarters: Sixola had telephoned once to say that cables had been sent to New York, to Scotland Yard, and to the sûretés of France, Italy, Turkey and the Balkan countries; the urgent Carlotta had paid a friendly visit to the Ministry of Sanitation, and Simmonds had been to a reception at the palace. The Carnation continued to cherish Simmonds as a butt for her not unkindly amusement, and the phlegmatic Hoffmann had been wisely unhelpful. Saturn and Sappho had learned to recognize Simmonds as a person they could trust to treat them respectfully.

On the evening of the première of *Leda* Simmonds had received his first mail from home: a bulky package of newspapers and a letter from a married niece. There had been a little rain in Mansfield but it was fine now: Mother had been asked to organize a stall for the bazaar, and Tom was hoping to go back to work next week. Simmonds would rather spend an evening with the London newspapers than watch the film for which two continents had waited. At a quarter to ten, when Pero and the others, after a festive dinner, had been gone little more than half an hour, the telephone buzzed. Simmonds pulled on his slippers, and shuffled across the room. It was Aubrey.

'Captain, art thou sleeping? No? Good. There's a little spot of bother here. The movies have refused to move, Pero's exploded, and everyone's asking each other what's happened.'

'Well, what has happened?'

'I'm not quite sure yet. Something's happened to *Leda*. I dashed first thing for the telephone. Wait a moment—there's Hoffmann—if you'll hold on, I'll . . .'

Simmonds, over the telephone, heard angry voices, and then as Aubrey didn't seem to come back he jammed on the receiver and reached for his boots.

At the Acropolis Cinema puzzled guests were wondering when the preliminary shorts were to come to an end. They had enjoyed two cartoons and endured two travelogues. They were aware of a long pause before the last one, and of a hurrying to and fro in the background. Pero's seat was vacant, for at that moment he was holding the second operator by the throat, while the other operator was dancing between the excited group by the door and his machines.

'We don't know anything about it, Señor Zaragoza, we

don't know anything about it,' the second operator kept gasping out, his eyes bulging. Aubrey, who had followed Hoffmann from the office where he had telephoned Simmonds to the door of the booth, slipped past Pero and regarded the cans of film strewn on the floor. Each round can contained a thousand feet of *Leda*, and each thousand feet was cut up into a thousand parts. The first operator was saying to nobody:

'They've been cut up with a razor. We didn't know a thing till we opened the first can. It was all right when we tried it through yesterday. The only thing is, we might be able to piece it together—that is if you don't get it out of order. It would take a couple of days. We didn't know a thing till we opened the first can. We didn't—'

'You know a thing now,' exploded Pero, dropping the second assistant and whirling his arms at the other. 'There's a thousand people there and a dozen of the biggest film men in the world, and they've come to see that film.'

'We could put on another one,' suggested the second assistant unwisely.

'I don't care what you do, you can do what you like. It is all up, I am ruined, I am made a fool.' Pero caught sight of Aubrey:

'And you—where is Simmonds, where are all the men for whom I pay. My theatre is burned down, my films are cut to pieces, where is he, what is he doing?'

Simmonds, at that moment, was ascending the iron steps towards the operating booth. It was no moment for his appearance, and Aubrey, on the look out, violently signalled him back. Luckily, Pero caught sight of Hoffmann's phlegmatic face, and disliked it. Aubrey swung down the steps, caught Simmonds by the arm and, drawing him into a corner, reported what had happened. Simmonds's brain was intermittent in its action, but it was clear now.

'Well,' he inquired, almost before Aubrey had finished, 'what about those men? Didn't you have any of your Sanitary Inspectors posted here?'

'Only one—the little fellow we called Alfred the Great— Alfredo.'

'Well, where is he? Hasn't he reported to you?'

'Have a heart. It's only four minutes since the first alarm. He's probably trying to find me—I fixed him up as supernumerary cloak-room attendant.'

'Let's find him.' Simmonds started to go.

The regular cloak-room attendant was discussing with the woman from the ladies' cloak-room the possible cause of the alarums and excursions. Tackled by Aubrey, he excitedly recollected that Alfredo hadn't turned up at all that evening.

'But, señor, I have managed alone until a few days ago, when Alfredo came to assist me. I thought he would not stay long, he did not understand the business. No, he said nothing about not coming tonight. He was here yesterday, and I have not seen him since.'

Simmonds drew Aubrey out of earshot:

'You'd better call up your headquarters and see if he's there.' Simmonds still called them 'your' headquarters. It was convenient to blame Aubrey at this moment. Pero and Hoffmann passed at the end of the corridor: the way to the operating box was clear. Simmonds left his rather crestfallen assistant abruptly.

In the operating booth the two men were still discussing the calamity while they threaded up the machine with a stop-gap film. Pero's tearful voice could be heard from the other end of the cinema as he made what excuses and explanations he could.

'Now,' Simmonds was stalwart and encouraging, 'just tell me exactly what you know.'

They hadn't much to tell: the film had been all right on the previous day, when they had tried it through. The film was stored in fireproof vaults, access to which was through the cloak-room. At this point Simmonds had made a quick movement of interest. There was a small lift, too small, Simmonds saw, for a human body, connecting the operating booth with the film vaults. During the afternoon both operators had arrived to run through the news-reel film which had only been received that day. Afterwards they had left the news-reel film in the vault and gone off for a drink before the evening performance. It was perfectly true, they had not bothered to lock up the vaults. The new cloak-room attendant, Alfredo, would be arriving for duty. He would be in the cloak-room, through which only was there access to the vaults. Alfredo had not been there on their return, when they had gone straight to the vaults and loaded the cans of film on to the lift. It was only upon opening the first can, a moment before it was required, that they had discovered the damage, and at once informed Señor Zaragoza.

Simmonds descended to look at the vaults, which told him little, for they had anyway been unlocked for several hours during the afternoon. Here Aubrey found him.

'No good. There's only one man there on duty, and he hasn't seen Alfredo since yesterday morning.'

'I didn't think he would have,' said Simmonds, outlining the new evidence. 'It looks as if Alfredo has been bribed, or something. If his body had been lying around it would have been found. Those operator fellows appear to be telling the truth—at any rate, we'll have to look after them later. We'd better go after Alfred the Great.'

Aubrey had the official car parked outside. He swung it down the fierce hairpins, Simmonds sitting beside him. They shot under arches and between high walls, and presently were rattling over the broken paving of the poorest quarter. Aubrey pulled up before a tall building to which odd little balconies clung like martens' nests in front of narrow windows.

'The House of the Virgin Margarita. Alfred the Great burns his cakes somewhere here.'

'We'll find him.'

They went together up a rickety staircase: an incurious family was eating its supper on the first landing.

'Alfredo?' inquired Aubrey. A man with a scarred face bit into an onion and pointed aloft:

'At the top.'

Simmonds's torch stabbed the darkness: they stumbled over a naked baby and a heap of garbage and arrived at last high above the world in an atmosphere it was possible to breathe. A partly open gallery, filled with washing, hung

over the rooftops, and offered a choice of half a dozen doors.
Aubrey beat on the first one.

'Alfredo?'

A woman's voice replied from the darkness:

'At the end—the little door with the broken handle.'

Simmonds got there first. There was a way of opening a
door into a dark room where danger might lurk, a way
which he had learned and Aubrey probably hadn't.

The room was almost dark, for the green sky of the last
light was rapidly turning to indigo. On the iron bedstead
lay Alfredo.

'Is he asleep?'

Aubrey was going forward to wake him, but Simmonds
gripped his arm:

'Steady a moment—it looks as if he was dead.'

## CHAPTER 12

### AN OLD EASTERN CUSTOM

Alfredo lay on the iron bedstead in his shirt and trousers.
It was difficult to tell whether he was *in* bed or not, for
the bedding consisted of a stained mattress and a twisted
blanket, and though he might be called dressed, he might
as easily be called undressed, for his jacket and socks and
shoes lay on a chair. There was an oil lamp on the table,
and Simmonds lit it and brought it near.

'Looks as if he had died in his sleep,' said Aubrey.

'Looks as if he had.' Simmonds turned over the body,
which was not yet quite rigid. There were no signs of violence
at all. Simmonds remarked on that.

'Only he died on the right day—for someone. If you see
what I mean.'

'I see what you mean.'

'Well, now, isn't it a good thing we've got a police surgeon all fixed up?' Aubrey was bright and busy. Even in San Rocco a death was sobering, and needed talking down. 'We'd better have Dr Falzego do a post-mortem.'

'All right. Get him.'

'I'll try and find someone to send.' Aubrey went out, and Simmonds carried the lamp around the room, looking at things. There was very little to look at. Besides the bed there were some shelves with dirty crockery, a table, the chair and an ant-eaten sideboard that had once been handsome. The drawers were stuffed with dirty clothes and the cupboards littered with old rubbish and mice droppings. There was some bread in a paper on one of the shelves, and several empty wine bottles. When Aubrey came back from his errand Simmonds was sniffing at the bottles.

'Found anything?'

'No.'

'It doesn't look,' said Aubrey, 'as if he committed suicide. I mean, there's no weapon—'

'And there's no wound.'

'No, no, of course not. And he isn't grasping the poison phial.'

'There wasn't any food near him. That bread hasn't been cut for a whole day at least, and these bottles were on the shelf. If he drank poison, it's funny he should want to put the bottles back on the shelf.'

'If it isn't suicide, or murder,' Aubrey calculated, 'then he died in his sleep. He wasn't very stiff, was he? That would make it during the siesta. He took off his shoes and socks, anyway, so when he lay down he wasn't feeling so ill as not to do that.'

Simmonds set the lamp back on the table:

'What about that girl, Margarita?'

'Margarita?'

'The one you talked to—the Virgin Margarita. You said this was her house.'

'Ah, that one. I don't think her name's Margarita, and I wouldn't swear to her qualifications. The House of the Virgin Margarita is the name of the house: some saint or something. At least, evidently, she was a saint—'

'Well, whoever she is or isn't, let's talk to that girl.'

They went out into the gallery among the washing and knocked on the door at the end. The girl they had spoken to before came out. It was dark there, and her room was in darkness. She stood near to them in a cotton dress, and she was warm with sleep. They couldn't tell how she felt about the death of Alfredo: she said she was sorry—just when he had honest work at the cinema, too. She had heard him pass her door at the time of the siesta, and she had not seen him since.

'And what about the other people who live up here?' Aubrey, who was interpreting for Simmonds, pointed to the other doors.

'No one. They are empty, as you may see for yourselves.'

'Ask the young lady if she has been in her room all the time since the siesta.'

Aubrey asked.

'She says she has. She does sewing. She worked till it was dark.'

'Ask her if she heard anyone else pass, except Alfredo.'

'She heard no one. She would have heard if anyone else had passed.'

'Why is she sure it was Alfredo she heard—did he speak to her?'

'Yes, she is sure it was Alfredo. It appears now that he shouted a pleasantry to her, because of her intimate washing which was hanging on the rails.'

The girl also told them that she had never known Alfredo to be ill.

Simmonds flashed his lamp into the other rooms. It wouldn't last a great deal longer, for he couldn't get a battery to fit it. But he did not have to waste the light to see that the other rooms were unoccupied. He was standing in the doorway of the last one when he suddenly became aware that someone was breathing close to him. Aubrey had gone back, on his own devices, to Alfredo's room. Simmonds swung round, and the pencil of light picked up a tall young man carrying something under his arm. Simmonds could see the white face, a vee of white shirt, his hands and white rubber shoes. The young man started back, and then broke out into rapid Spanish. Simmonds recognized the word 'photograph,' and then Aubrey came to make introductions. This was the official criminal photographer. He thought he had better send for him too. He had a little studio near the docks where he took passport photos, and photos on porcelain decorated with shells. These could be seen on every decent grave in the cemetery beyond the old arsenal. The tall youth and Aubrey encouraged each other in the important business of setting up the camera and burning magnesium ribbon, while the inhabitants of the house, at last waking up to the fact that something interesting had happened, began to cluster in the gallery. They were all sorry about Alfredo but very reserved. A disturbance lower down the stairs announced another arrival—Dr Falzego, evidently, for the important-looking man walked straight through the murmuring spectators to Simmonds, with an air of authority and of annoyance. Aubrey had told Simmonds that Dr Falzego had several American degrees: that he was a first-class surgeon, but that there had been a scandal, or something. He had one of those too dominating personalities, which put Simmonds on the defensive, but, watching him at work, Simmonds had to admit that he knew his business. Two of Aubrey's sanitary inspectors had by this time arrived. Aubrey had sent for them at the same time as he had sent for the photographer, and they were keeping back the spectators. It did not seem to take Dr Falzego long to arrive at an opinion. It was disappointingly negative:

'He died about nine hours ago. Shock, heart failure—a stroke. Those are the symptoms.'

'You can't find any wound?'

'There is no wound.'

'Poison?'

Falzego shrugged:

'It doesn't look like it. But it may be. You can send the body to the Public Hospital, and ring me up tomorrow. I won't promise you anything—I've got no help there, no proper equipment. You understand that?'

'Quite.' Simmonds could be brisk too. 'We can't help you —we can't tell you what to look for, but this man died at an extremely convenient time for some person.'

Falzego left them abruptly, and Aubrey started to organize the removal of the body. Aubrey's fertile invention might have led Simmonds farther than he wanted to go, but the young man was imperturbably practical when it came to dealing with problems of this sort. What he didn't know he made up as he went along. He had the ruling class attitude, and that Simmonds had never possessed.

'The doctor was pretty snappy,' Aubrey observed when they had nothing to do but await the arrival of a stretcher. 'Definitely non-San Roccan.'

'Well, I'm not San Roccan, am I?' inquired Simmonds. 'Nor you, either.'

'No, we aren't. And that's hard on the San Roccans. I mean, all these foreigners buzzing round and taking notice. It's tough on them. Soon it won't be a land fit for murderers. I wonder if we're not making a nuisance of ourselves.'

A deputation consisting of Hoffmann came to Simmonds the next morning:

'Señor Zaragoza would like to see you, Mr Simmonds, if you're not too busy.'

Simmonds thought that probably Pero did want to see him. His stock, he imagined, might be slumping at the moment. He was pretty used to gauging the rise and fall of his stock, and used to having his answer ready.

Pero, in silk pyjamas, was walking up and down smoking a cigarette. Simmonds reported.

'The day you come—a fire; now more sabotage. That film cannot be replaced. It was not a matter of a thousand dollars or of ten thousand, perhaps the whole history of San Rocco has been altered. Big executives from Hollywood have wasted their time, they think I am a fraud, a man of nothing. And you—I bring you from England, I make you important. You have everything you ask for—the man Wilkinson, a car, a force of detectives. You find one of them dead, you do not even know how he died. All you know is

93

that you think there is a man with a big head. Consider if it is not your head that is big.'

This had never been the way to speak to Simmonds, but he was at a disadvantage now because his favourite card, resignation, couldn't be played. One of his men, one of the sanitary inspectors, and it didn't make any difference that Simmonds had been opposed to the idea of employing them, had died, had been murdered, probably, on duty. Simmonds couldn't walk out till that man had been avenged. He looked at Pero stolidly:

'I didn't ask for Wilkinson, Mr Saratoga.'

'You said you couldn't act without help.'

'I said I didn't see what I could do, and asked to be released. And you suggested I should have help. I oughtn't to have given in. But I'm not being dictated to by you now —it's gone beyond that. There's a poor fellow been killed. That's more important than any of your troubles. You know your own business best—' Simmonds's tone grew truculent —'but it strikes me you're getting a lot of publicity. Steamship sailings to San Rocco jumped fifteen per cent after the fire, because San Rocco was in the news, and whether I find anything, or whether I don't, it strikes me that a Scotland Yard detective is damned good publicity—same as those two tigers and that girl.'

Pero had begun by gesturing Simmonds to stop, his face working, but when Simmonds didn't stop he became calm, and then he began to smile.

'Mr Simmonds, you are very clever. I prepared a lecture for you, and you have taken the offensive.' He looked at Simmonds, who had grown a little red, wisely and with charm. 'Do you think that I am like the actress who steals her own jewels for the sake of publicity? My friend, that publicity was never yet worth while. The newspapers will print such a story only because that actress is big enough to be already interesting to the public. Such publicity does not make her any bigger, it only shows that she is big.'

Simmonds at that moment was convinced of Pero's honesty. Afterwards he remembered that Pero's simile hadn't proved anything, and that he had become suddenly friendly when he had every right to become angry. He shared his suspicions with Aubrey, who agreed. They were on their way to the Public Hospital, for Simmonds had begun to fidget, and he couldn't wait for Dr Falzego's report.

'It's a pretty idea,' said Aubrey, 'and if you find that Alfredo was murdered by hirelings of Pero so that he shouldn't be on duty when they'd planned to visit the film vaults, and if in the end you have to arrest Pero, at what point would Pero stop paying us? It isn't ethical for us to take his money.'

Simmonds grunted.

'It seems strange, now I come to think of it,' Aubrey continued, 'that the operators left the vault unlocked. But, of course,' he conceded fairly, 'that doesn't mean they were told to do so by Pero.'

Simmonds didn't care about Aubrey theorizing while he was at the wheel of the car. Already they had driven a market cart on to the pavement and met a herd of goats at a blind corner. Now they took an alarming turn through a narrow yellow archway and drew up at the main doorway of the Public Hospital. Inside there was the authentic odour, and, from what Simmonds could see, up-to-date equipment.

'Yes, it's rather a show-piece.' Aubrey, as usual, could give the low-down. 'A hundred beds, and the patients can be killed off in any of the most modern experimental ways they like. After the first hundred, all the other cases in San Rocco just die at home. No real San Roccan would come here—voluntarily. It's run by foreign charities, and the San Roccans rather resent it.'

Falzego met them at the door of the post-mortem room: he had not slept, his eyes were bright and his fingers vivid with nicotine. Aubrey looked round the room, and then hastily kept his eyes on Dr Falzego.

'What luck?' demanded Simmonds.

Perhaps the suggestion of chance offended Falzego, for he answered obliquely:

'I will tell you what I've done. The man had taken his boots and socks off, and lain down to sleep. That suggested a poison. I have carried out tests of the stomach contents.

Also of the intestines and liver. The liver—' he held up a glass jar and subjected it to a look of searching disapproval —'is small and fatty. But nothing out of the way. All the normal tests for poisons have failed. As there were no signs of contusion or bleeding, I then considered the possibility that he was throttled. There were no external marks, but it was just possible none had been left—skilful manipulation sometimes doesn't, if, as we could suppose in this case, the subject was sleeping.' The doctor passed, as if this idea was still attractive. Simmonds nodded:

'Yes, dislocation of the neck. I've met pretty cases of that.'

'But we must abandon the idea. See, I've opened up the trachea and the oesophagus—right down to the thorax. I might have saved myself the trouble. I've taken a look at the spinal canal—no disturbance, no dislocation. In fact, there's every indication that the man died—well, from heart disease. That might be in the heart—though it looks well enough, or it might be from the brain—a clot on the brain, a stroke, paralysis.'

Dr Falzego bit his nails nervously: the over-impressive manner had left him, and he spoke like a man angry with himself. Simmonds waited impassively, it wasn't for him to help out the expert. Aubrey, however, was not so patient. He hovered round the table with its unpleasant burden, and at the word 'brain' noticeably perked up.

'The brain? Something might have happened to the brain?' he echoed. Falzego was purposelessly shaking up some of his jars and test-tubes. 'That might be an idea,' Aubrey continued, working out his thoughts aloud. 'There really might be something in that.' Suddenly he turned to the doctor: 'You haven't shaved the head?'

'Shaved the head? If you think he has a bullet in his brain—' Falzego did not continue to examine the absurdity.

'Short hair—you'd see anything like that,' Simmonds reminded Aubrey.

'No, I wasn't thinking of bullets . . .' Aubrey stared at the close-cropped hair, and then gingerly took up a blunt probe which lay on the table. 'Some of Pero's unknowns came from the East, so perhaps . . .'

96

Simmonds had made half a step forward as if to stop Aubrey from interfering with the specialist's job. The doctor watched with the dawning of a contemptuous smile.

'Dr Falzego—' Aubrey spoke quietly, but there was the lilt of triumph in his voice. 'Did you notice this—' Falzego moved forward. Aubrey was pointing with the probe to something so minute that Simmonds, coming up behind, could see nothing.

'What is it? I can't see anything.'

Aubrey was content to wait there, with the probe still pointing to that invisible something while Falzego, suddenly vital again, fetched some fine tweezers from his instrument case.

'It's just there—' Aubrey began helpfully.

'Yes, yes—I can see—' the doctor motioned him away.

'It was the brain which gave me the idea—and those men coming from the East . . .' Aubrey almost apologetically murmured, as Simmonds craned forward to see the small bright object which Falzego suddenly held up to the light on the end of the tweezers.

It was a small piece of pointed steel, the end, perhaps, of a darning needle.

'Yes, that could kill him—' Falzego dropped it into a watch-glass. 'It was in the right part of the brain, and it would have that effect. Instant death. It left no more blood than a bug-bite. But—' he turned to Aubrey—'he didn't drive it in himself, and how anyone else could do it, I don't see.'

'I believe it's a nice operation.' Aubrey had been holding himself in, but he was obviously enjoying himself. 'It's an old Eastern custom, but, of course, it may have spread to San Rocco, the world's such a small place nowadays. You have a wooden club, shaped at the end something like a spoon, and weighted. There's a steel needle set in at exactly the right place, and if you're of championship status the needle comes away again. You definitely get disqualified if it breaks off and part gets left behind. It's a beautiful system, but it needs nerve and skill, and you must have plenty of time to aim. But poor Alfredo was probably sleeping like a log.'

Simmonds was observing Aubrey with a bleak eye:

'You seem to know a lot about it.'

'Oh, I've mixed in very strange company in my time,' said Aubrey jauntily. 'You'd be surprised how much I know.'


# CHAPTER 13

## EVERYTHING BECOMES EASY

Simmonds had no objection to Aubrey taking along a bag containing finger-print apparatus to the House of the Virgin. Several sanitary inspectors, whose strange and interesting new occupation, however, was by this time well known to the underworld, had been placed on guard, with general orders to find out what they could find out. The warren-like building had a bad reputation: the girl to whom they had spoken, her name was Juana, had no reputation at all.

'The question is,' Simmonds worried, as they drove towards the house, 'was she telling the truth when she said no one passed along the gallery after Alfredo?'

'She may believe,' Aubrey said judicially, 'that no one else did pass, but someone else may have passed, and she may have been sleeping. Roughly, I think she thought she was telling the truth.'

'I know. But supposing no one did pass along the gallery, then they either levitated themselves, or dropped from a balloon. Or, of course, climbed up the outside of the house.'

'The last idea's feasible.'

'Then we'll see if it's possible.'

Alfredo's window was small, and below it the wall fell straight down for fifty feet.

'Stumped, by gad!' exclaimed Aubrey.

'Let's look at the other side.' Simmonds led the way, and

peered over the insecure railing which ran along the gallery. The wall here was more broken, there were projecting balconies and ledges, but below there was a busy courtyard, now full of interested spectators, and unlikely, even in the middle of the day, to be entirely deserted.

'The only thing is—the empty rooms. A man might hide there both before and after, and there may be some way of reaching them apart from the gallery.'

'They have no message for me,' Aubrey said disappointedly, when they had examined three of them and were on the point of entering the fourth. Simmonds humphed, and crossed to the window. It was a large window with many broken panes and rotting woodwork. Simmonds suddenly swooped.

'Eureka!' Aubrey exclaimed. 'Or rather, since you did the finding, it should be . . . never mind what it should be, I've forgotten my Greek.'

'What?'

'I said I'd forgotten my Greek.'

'I don't know what you're talking about—'

'Well, never mind. The thing you're excited about is that splinter?'

The splinter which Simmonds was holding had evidently been broken off from the rotting window frame, and recently, for the dry, spongy wood was white and fresh where it was broken. Below this window the pan-tiled roof of a penthouse reached to within three feet of the sill, and below the penthouse a system of roofs, balconies and other coigns of vantage reached to the ground level.

'I'll admit that may come in useful at last,' Simmonds said handsomely, as Aubrey produced a camel-hair brush and some grey powder and began painting over the window-frame. As he watched Aubrey at work, childishly enthusiastic, or, anyway, seeming to be that, it was not entirely absent from Simmonds's thoughts that Aubrey himself might be connected in some way with the events they were investigating. One of the unknowns was an Englishman. It was possible that Aubrey was now thirty—he might even be more—and that made him, ten years ago, of an age not impossible for the rôle. Or, it was an attractive idea, Aubrey might be the son of Gabriel Edward Hicks, a son taking vengeance for his father. In spite of his chatter, Aubrey revealed very little about himself, and the chatter might be in itself a smoke-screen. The various acts of sabotage might even, from their childish inventiveness, be the acts of a man with an undergraduate mind. The murder of Alfredo, alone, was out of character, but Aubrey might employ agents who had exceeded their orders. And it didn't exactly contribute to his innocence that he had jumped so quickly to that old eastern custom by which Alfredo had died.

These thoughts recurred later in the day, when Simmonds was sitting in the office where—was it, after all, by coincidence?—he had met Aubrey for the first time. Aubrey was sitting opposite to him, engrossed in the labelling and numbering of an assorted collection of finger-prints which he had found in the House of the Virgin. They had been photographed by the lank youth with the plimsolls. Aubrey must have felt the eyes of Simmonds upon him, for he looked up and for a moment his grey innocent eyes were held by those of Simmonds, which were blue and hard and sagacious. Often Simmonds had based a whole campaign upon the impression afforded by such an interchange of glances. But Aubrey's still baffled him: there had been something sad, unfathomable, almost piteous, in that unveiled look. But it was only for a moment: Aubrey's protective colouring, the fool, was immediately resumed:

'Name the detective's greatest enemies in two words: Vim and gloves.'

That was so weak that the need for something to break momentary tension was all the more clearly seen. But the tension was more completely broken the next minute, for there was a knock on the door and one of the sanitary inspectors appeared importantly:

'His Excellency the Chief of Police wishes to see you, Captain and sir.'

Simmonds brushed pipe ash from his creased tweed suit as Sixola entered, resplendent in uniform.

100

'This time,' he said agreeably, 'I call upon you. I have very good news.' He accepted a chair, beaming upon them. 'My dear sir, your search is now made very much more narrow. I have a communication from the chief of police in Angora. Both Cirilo Redoza and the Armenian, Anouzin, were executed five years ago for complicity in anti-national propaganda. What that exactly means I do not know, and we do not need to ask. The fact remains that they are undoubtedly dead. Your labours are now reduced to tracing only one man.'

'The Englishman?'

'Exactly.'

Simmonds found that his glance in Aubrey's direction was duplicated by one on the part of Sixola. Aubrey quite excitedly jumped up:

'Gabriel Hicks!'

'I had forgotten his name.' Sixola, still smiling, dusted his gold lace.

'Well, then—' Aubrey's further excited remark was interrupted by the reappearance of the sanitary inspector who had announced Sixola. This time he beckoned to Aubrey. Simmonds followed that young man with his eyes, as with an excuse, he left the room. Then he turned to find himself the object of Sixola's amused scrutiny.

'It is very curious,' Sixola remarked, 'that an English detective, with an English lieutenant, should find themselves in San Rocco engaged in tracing an English criminal. There are not so many English persons in the island. You should have quick success. I wish it to you.'

Half Simmonds's attention was directed to the door, from the other side of which came the voice of Aubrey and several sanitary inspectors. Sixola droned on with hopeful generalizations: he seemed to be well informed about everything Simmonds had been doing, and his compliments were double-edged with jealousy. After ten minutes of this a not-responsive Simmonds escorted him to the door. Aubrey and the inspectors had vanished, but Sixola's too military looking car had hardly departed when Aubrey emerged from the big room on the ground floor, which had been turned into a sort of guard-room, with an expression of suppressed excitement. The story he had to tell he would not begin till they were seated again in the office.

'It's something definite at last!' Even at his most excited, Aubrey had to chatter. 'At least, I think so. On the other hand—well, you must judge. As you suggested, I sent round a gang of men to call at all the chemists' shops. Of course—' Aubrey was off at a tangent—'the man may have invented it —for the sake of the little reward of fifty dollars I offered. If we pay it, that means two carboys of disinfecting fluid.'

Admirable patience kept Simmonds from violence.

'It's the fellow with the nose on one side. Um . . . well, never mind his name. This star turn has found a chemist's shop in Hortaleza, the high-class suburb and bathing beach to the east of the town, where the chemist remembers supplying a rather disreputable San Roccan with some permanganate crystals. He remembered it because his clients are mostly the well-to-do people from the neighbouring villas. And also because—' Aubrey paused impressively —'he found later in the day that a bottle of toilet glycerine was missing from the counter!'

Simmonds did not look at Aubrey: it simply wasn't possible that his theory was going to be proved. He wondered if Aubrey hadn't staged this proof, not, he now thought, from ulterior motives, but because he was a crazy fool playing an elaborate game of make-believe. But there was just the possibility that his theory had been right, that the comic organization had stumbled on something. He could hardly refuse to accompany Aubrey to Hortaleza, but he went with misgivings.

A shady boulevard led out of the town at the east, and there, on the edge of the bathing beach, was a little suburban pharmacy. Its windows were full of rubber horses and kodaks, but drugs were sold too. The owner was not unprepared for their arrival. His manner was important enough to be genuine. He took them into the little back dispensing-room and rattled away in voluble Spanish, which Simmonds could not follow, and into which Aubrey, also not entirely following, interjected a succession of *hombres* and *es veros*.

When this was all over he sat back, and was prepared to answer questions.

'Ask him if he saw what the man was like?'

'He says the man was like a bandit, a robber. He says nothing about a big head.'

'Was he short?'

'He was either short or tall, he says.'

'And he purchased permanganate of potash, and afterwards the bottle of glycerine was missing?'

'Yes. He says he had exactly ten bottles displayed in a pyramid on the counter, and when he came to rearrange the counter in the evening the top bottle was missing.'

'Ask him if he would be able to identify the man if he saw him again.'

This question led to another speech on the part of the pharmacist, during the course of which Simmonds caught the word 'auto' repeated several times.

'We're in luck!' Aubrey passed on the good news. 'The man went away in an auto—an old American car. Señor Lizarda's wife thinks the car was a two-seater Willard.'

'And *she* noticed the make of the car, no doubt, because desperadoes, who may be either short or tall and steal bottles of glycerine, do not usually possess autos?'

Aubrey regarded Simmonds with a hurt expression:

'You don't believe in fairies, do you?'

'I'll believe in this lead enough to follow it up,' Simmonds agreed grudgingly. 'Only it's all too good to be true. And I'm not sure that the reward hasn't been father to the information, in this case.'

Simmonds rather preferred bad fortune to good fortune, because bad fortune was an excuse and good fortune a responsibility. All the same, he had risen, and now moved towards a telephone cabinet in the shop.

'The Ministry of the Interior, please,' he demanded, and then proved that he had been acquainting himself with knowledge generally useful to detectives by asking for the auto registration department. Aubrey, before the number was secured, plucked his sleeve:

'I wish you'd let me do that. I know the secretary of the little retired major who is supposed to run the department.'

'Doesn't he run it, then?'

'Oh, yes, but the whole thing's a ramp. Half the car owners arrange with him for an official permit, which is free, and he takes a small consideration per cubic centimetre of cylinder capacity. Or, at least, the secretary gets it in the end. She has a golden voice and a figure like a—'

'Half a moment, please.' Simmonds handed the receiver to Aubrey. 'The golden voice.'

A pleasant minute was spent by Aubrey as he inquired as to the health of the golden voice, and passed on to various other international passports to good humour. Simmonds had done the same himself on occasions in the service of the British public, and he waited indulgently. Aubrey made signs for him to be ready with paper and pencil. By the time he had hung up there was a list of seven names and addresses of owners of Willard cars.

'That doesn't include,' Aubrey explained, 'the holders of official permits. She can't get that list till the Major wakes up.' Aubrey studied Simmonds's note-book. 'Well, we can rule out all those with two letters in the registration number to start with. It was an old car, and the two-letter numbers didn't start till this year.'

Simmonds struck out four names.

'You can strike out the first name, temporarily at all events, it belongs to a deputy, and the last one belongs to a dentist. And dentists don't commit crimes—they have sufficient outlet for their subliminal desires.'

'That'll pass for reasoning at the moment. So we'll make a first call upon—' Simmonds had only two to choose from —'Carlos Garcia.'

'Why him rather than the other one?'

'Because Garcia lives farther away from here. It stands to reason a man would choose a shop where he wasn't known, as far from his own district as possible.'

Aubrey turned the car, and they speeded back along the boulevard, threaded the town, and penetrated into the forest on the other side. Soon the trees grew more sparsely, and

they climbed broken hills, jolted over a level-crossing of the
Grand Central Railway, and arrived at last, directed by
peasants, at a shabby-looking group of buildings, insuffi-
ciently roofed with corrugated iron and surrounded by ill-
kept plantations. The car bumped over the dusty courtyard
of hard earth, and they got out and walked in the burning
sun of late afternoon towards the main building. Simmonds
was aware of the danger, they were many yards from cover,
and the little windows of the broken down buildings squinted
at them hostilely. On Simmonds's part courage was bred
from sloth, and on Aubrey's, for he walked along chirpily,
from foolhardiness. The main door was open, and the interior invitingly cool. They walked in. A short, shabbily
dressed man with a big head and a shock of black hair
turned slowly from the fire on which smoked an iron pot of
greasy stew. Simmonds halted and tipped back his bowler
hat.

'Are you,' he inquired, and he might only have been
interested in a minor motoring offence, 'the owner of a
two-seater Willard car, number V 157?'


## CHAPTER 14

## THE METHODS OF THE ENGLISH


The man with the big head straightened up and regarded
them with some preoccupation of his own. The room in
which they stood was not that of a peasant, it was a civilized
room diseased with poverty. The man was like that too.
Then the fellow seemed to collect himself; he took a step
forward with a casual:

'Yes, it's outside. Come this way.'

It was the most natural movement in the world, and it
nearly succeeded, but as Garcia stretched out for the gun
which was leaning against the wall Aubrey's leg shot out.

Garcia tripped, the gun fell down and Simmonds's big arms closed round him.

'Neat!' Aubrey picked up Simmonds's bowler hat and blew on it.

'For heaven's sake get that gun out of the way.' Simmonds had strong arms and a text-book grip, but Garcia was powerful also. Suddenly he ceased to struggle. Simmonds cautiously ran his hands up and down; no weapons. Garcia maintained a sulky silence, which was not a bad card for him to play, but showed that he knew what they were there for.

'Garcia, I arrest you for being illegally concerned in setting fire to a certain building, namely the Acropolis Theatre.'

The formula rang strangely, but Simmonds was punctilious.

'You needn't warn him about anything he may say being taken down,' Aubrey put in hastily, 'we don't do that here —I mean, we don't warn suspected persons.'

'He's not saying anything, anyhow,' Simmonds grunted, taking Garcia by the arm. 'Come on, you're coming back with us.'

Aubrey drove back to town. Garcia, sitting beside Simmonds who was alert for any surprise movement, continued to say nothing. At headquarters their arrival was triumphant: eight sanitary inspectors, gambling their pay on the doorstep, were engaged in repartee with some creole girls of the neighbourhood, who, fortified by daylight and numbers, were not at a loss in the battle of witty improprieties. As the car stopped the men sprang up, glad perhaps that an end had been put to a game in which they were the more vulnerable.

'An arrest!'

'The murderer of Alfredo!'

'The fire bug!'

The excitement buzzed. Garcia was handed over, still saying nothing, to a selected guard, and Aubrey asked Simmonds rather helplessly what they were to do next. Simmonds had been wondering this all the way along in the car. Having got his suspect he had to invent a whole machinery for dealing with him. Or hand him over to Sixola. And that Simmonds stubbornly didn't wish to do.

'We'll see if he won't talk, now that he sees we mean business,' Simmonds pronounced at last. 'Have him brought up here.'

It was a little difficult to make Garcia understand that he ought to answer questions, yet he accepted the authority of his questioners. He withdrew behind the veil of language, looking blank very often when Simmonds spoke, and less excusably when Aubrey took over the questioning. He reiterated that he knew nothing about the fire, that at the time of the fire he was at his farm, and that he had never purchased anything at the Hortaleza pharmacy.

'Now listen,' Simmonds changed his tone, 'we know a great deal more than you think. But it isn't you we're after primarily. We want to know who you were working for and who paid you.' He went on to offer an immediate release for this information, and when Garcia for a moment appeared to hesitate, pressed in with questions again. But a time arrived when it was dangerous to continue, as the weakness of their position began to be revealed.

'We'll have to put him in cold storage till we can face him with the chemist, that French dancer and with the Carnation,' Simmonds said aside to Aubrey in English.

'What about—' Aubrey had been waiting for this moment —'what about taking his tabs?'

'If you like.' Simmonds waved over the prisoner, who, upon seeing Aubrey open up the ink pad and set out the forms he had had printed, visibly reacted. For a moment it looked as if he were going to refuse.

'Of course, if you don't know anything about anything,' Aubrey suggested kindly, 'there can't be any point in being stubborn. And we shall be able to pick up some very nice prints from your house.'

Garcia suddenly pressed his broad blunt thumb upon the pad and squeezed it on to the paper. He followed with the fingers, his willingness even disconcerting.

'All right.' Simmonds had watched him without comment. 'Now send him downstairs again. Give him some food if he wants it.'

While Aubrey was executing this Simmonds had some telephone calls: to the chemist, to Calcagno at the theatre to ask if the girl Emilienne was still available, and to the Carnation. The Carnation's voice over the telephone was unexpectedly businesslike:

'I don't know whether I shall be able to recognize the man, but I will come, of course. I was thinking about you only an hour ago, and wondering how you were getting on.'

Five minutes later, when Simmonds was still debating whether the Carnation's endearing farewell had been spoken with her tongue in her cheek, Pero rang up. Simmonds realized with a shock that he had forgotten about Pero, which showed how far he had gone since he first arrived in San Rocco. In fact, he no longer looked upon himself as Pero's private detective but as a public servant of San Rocco, chief of the Criminal Investigation Department. Circumstances and Aubrey had been too much for him.

Pero, of course, had heard about the arrest from the Carnation, who must have rung him up immediately upon hearing from Simmonds. Interesting reflections upon this fact were interrupted by the return of Aubrey, who carried a still dripping photographic print.

'It's the one from the House of the Virgin, from the frame of the window. I don't trust myself, but I'd take a small bet that they're identical with the ones we've just taken— Garcia's. What does the expert think?'

'To start with I'm not an expert,' said Simmonds, but good humouredly, taking out the steel rimmed spectacles he seldom used. Almost benevolent in these, he drew the prints towards him. He couldn't call himself an expert—he had had a general grounding in the principles and that was all.

'They may be the same,' he admitted finally.

'If they are the same—then you'll charge him with the murder of Alfredo?'

Simmonds locked the prints in a drawer and stood up without a direct answer:

'I've fixed the identity parade for seven o'clock, so that the Carnation can come on her way to the theatre. You'll have to fetch the chemist, and you'll have to arrange for the blanks. Better get a dozen.'

'And that won't take long. We'll be fair, and I'll try and match him up—not that that will be difficult, one San Roccan is very much like another San Roccan.' Aubrey paused in the doorway, with a disarming change of mood: 'You know, I've been rushing at this thing as if it was a first-class game, but I do also think what will happen to that man if he is found guilty.'

'He killed Alfredo,' Simmonds said stoutly, but with the same misgivings.

'Yes, quite.' Aubrey still hesitated. 'In England, well, of course, it would be regrettably anti-social to want to let the fellow off. But here—murder doesn't seem so anti-social somehow. However—I'm rather glad about it—the San Roccans abolished capital punishment twenty years ago. So I suppose—well, I'll be seeing about things.'

Simmonds also was ill at ease. But he was committed now, he had to go on, to win his case, or to look a fool. And Simmonds had no intention of letting that happen.

The identity parade was almost a social occasion. The Carnation, although she was dressed simply, as good taste suggested, could not avoid looking glamorous. Pero and Calcagno arrived with the French dancer: the chemist brought his wife and several relations. Aubrey, in spite of his confession of weakness, warmed up to his part as master of ceremonies, running up and down, bearing messages and instructing the blanks not to indicate their innocence in any way. It was not very easy to arrange that none of the witnesses should communicate together before being ushered into the guard-room, where a dozen labelled San Roccans were kept walking up and down. Everything was to be done with strict fairness, and an hour later, when it was all over, when the visitors had gone, when the blanks had been paid off, and Garcia had consented to take some food, Simmonds and Aubrey wondered if they hadn't overdone it. The results were conflicting. Pero, to start with, could not pick out any of them as a man he had ever seen. That was unimportant. The Carnation, who had had the best view of the alleged Garcia, had selected two men, and hesitated so long between them that her final choice of a man who was not Garcia was not conclusive. Emilienne had immediately pointed out Garcia, but then had drawn back and refused to confirm her choice. All she would say was that she couldn't be certain. The chemist, on the other hand, had chosen at once and correctly. That proved, at any rate, that Garcia had been the man who had purchased permanganate of potash. That didn't make him a murderer, didn't even necessarily make him the fire-bug, without some more definite proof. The finger-prints were equally unsatisfactory. The photograph was blurred and fragmentary. Simmonds, as he weighed the evidence, recollected the advice which the Carnation had given him upon leaving:

'If he won't answer your questions, is it so difficult to make him?'

'Make him?' Simmonds had been cold.

'Only a guilty man is silent, I think. You should have no qualms in using persuasive methods.'

'That's not the way we do it,' Simmonds had priggishly replied. But now—he began to wonder. And the presence of Garcia had become a problem. Simmonds had hoped to find some definite evidence before nightfall, for Garcia couldn't be kept at the Ministry of Sanitation. Aubrey said that the only thing to do was to hand him over to the prison authorities. And that, as it turned out, was not so easy. To begin with, there was a considerable crowd to watch the departure of the car bearing Simmonds, Aubrey, Garcia and the most trusted of the inspectors. It was not an enthusiastic crowd: the popularity of the English detectives had waned a little: the people were beginning to ask each other what was wrong with their own police that they couldn't attend to all matters of public interest. If, queried some, what happened to the Acropolis *was* a matter of public interest. They forgot that Pero's venture brought tourists to the island and money to their pockets: they suspected, they did not quite understand how, that San Rocco was no longer their own: their civilization was threatened by the restless world.

The prison of San Rocco was a sixteenth-century Spanish fort, picturesque and insanitary—Aubrey could vouch for that. The prison and its inhabitants were not regarded with horror and moral nervousness, but with a sort of warm interest. Pious women brought food for the poor prisoners and said prayers for them in the neighbouring Jesuit church. Their friends came and chatted with them through the bars. In the old humane way life for the convicts was brutal but full of interesting diversities, the very smells were warm and full of life, little drawings remained for a hundred years on the stone walls, and their sentences were regarded as that expiatory punishment which is so much more satisfactory to the soul than scientific reform.

Simmonds thought the place looked old-fashioned. He jangled the bell, and when a turnkey appeared explained in his best Spanish that they had a prisoner to entrust to the care of the governor. The turnkey replied that he had not been expecting a prisoner, but that if he could see the official order he would be delighted to oblige.

'There isn't exactly an official order, but the man is here, and you know who I am, don't you?'

'Certainly, that is well known. But you see how I am placed. There is so much talk of economy that I must be careful whom I admit. Every rascal cannot be given a bed at the expense of the state.'

'Very well then, I'll see the governor.'

The turnkey was still hesitating when Aubrey joined Simmonds in the carved doorway. A dirty dollar note changed hands, and the turnkey retired, shutting the door against them.

'He'll go to the governor, all right, but I believe we've put our foot in it by arresting Garcia,' Aubrey said in a whisper. 'If we're not careful there'll be trouble.'

The turnkey reappeared more quickly than they had expected, and beckoned them to follow across the paved yard to the governor's office. That gentleman, stout, bearded and in a uniform which he was still buttoning up, started off by a refusal to receive the prisoner: he was sorry, but there was not a vacant cell. Aubrey unluckily knew that only condemned prisoners had cells, those awaiting trial lived in common, and as the courts had been sitting recently there must be accommodation. The governor, preoccupied and worried, ceased to argue that point. He did not deny that Simmonds had been given the necessary powers of arrest.

'His Excellency Don Miguel will be most displeased,' Aubrey took good care to point out.

'Yes, yes . . .' The governor was a troubled man. 'But his Excellency is not the chief of the police.'

They both understood suddenly that Sixola was at the bottom of the difficulty. Perhaps he was making it awkward for them on purpose.

'The great thing,' Aubrey suggested, tactfully not referring to the name which had been all but spoken, 'is to find a formula. Now, if you were to be out playing cards with some friends, and if the ·turnkey was to misunderstand your orders . . . well, the governor of a prison must relax sometimes, and it is very easy for a misunderstanding to arise. Tonight it is the turnkey who is responsible, and tomorrow morning the responsibility can be shifted on to the shoulders of Don Miguel.'

The governor lightened, then composed his face, and muttering some excuse left them. They sat in silence for ten minutes, Aubrey enjoying some inward amusement, and Simmonds chewing over the circumstances that were involving a disgruntled ex-detective in politics. He thought it was hard on him. When the governor continued not to return, Aubrey at last went out into the courtyard. Hearing voices, Simmonds stumped out into the moonlight.

'This gentleman,' Aubrey informed him with a wink, indicating the turnkey, 'tells me that the governor has been out all evening at the house of a friend, and that he himself has been in bed with stomach-ache. In his absence his wife has admitted the suspect Garcia, and she is entirely responsible for this act. Not, however, having any official status, the good woman will not be punished very severely.'

'I don't like to think of that at all,' said Simmonds.

'Oh, it will all be in the family. Her husband can beat her, and that will be good for her and a pleasure for him.'

## CHAPTER 15

## A TRIAL FOR SIMMONDS

The three examining magistrates, wearing red sashes and evening dress, took their seats. An official read from a paper:

'In the name of the Republic of San Rocco, silence. The magistrates of the people of San Rocco consider the case of Carlos Garcia, accused of theft and of feloniously setting fire to the Acropolis Theatre.'

The preliminary examination had at last begun after much ringing of telephones, of consultations and conferences. The wife of the turnkey had been censured and probably beaten, but Don Miguel's support of Simmonds had been sufficient to uphold the arrest. Pero had seemed pleased, and Carlotta had been urgent with congratulations. Simmonds, however, had a headache.

The bubble of talk subsided as Garcia appeared from a doorway and was escorted to a chair at the side of his counsel, a thin restless man in a gown, white bands and a flat black cap.

'Who bears witness against this man?' demanded the chief magistrate. Simmonds was nudged by the pleasant-looking rascal, also in gown and bands, who represented the prosecution. He stood up:

'I do.'

He was quite able to face the stares of the court, and his ordeal was short. He sat down again, according to the coaching he had received. The pleasant looking rascal presented the case. Simmonds could not follow all that he was saying, he caught the leading words—glycerine, rat,

Emilienne Sarell, Lizarda. Instead, he watched the faces of the magistrates and of Garcia. The prisoner listened carefully without betraying any emotion. Still Simmonds could not decide whether he was guilty or not. For the first quarter of an hour the magistrates took copious notes, and when they stopped Simmonds wondered uneasily if the faltering of the prosecutor was due to that fact. There was a pause at one time while affidavits of the witnesses—those who had attended the identity parade, Simmonds and Aubrey—were presented. This was the custom, and the magistrates had already received copies. The counsel had indeed then whispered an encouraging word, but in his following peroration all his shouting and the raising of his hands to heaven only revealed how much he had lost confidence.

When, after a short consultation among the magistrates, the chief of them began to speak, Simmonds was aware from the expression on the face of Garcia, and of his own man, that things were not going well for the prosecution. The magistrate spoke slowly and distinctly and Simmonds could follow enough of his speech to be ready for the summary whispered a moment later by his counsel.

'He says that the theory of the cause of the fire is most interesting, but that it lacks proof. He says even if the rat was soaked in glycerine, there is nothing to connect the rat with the fire.'

Simmonds nodded: he had been prepared to hear this. The magistrate recommenced. Simmonds, used by this time to the pitch of his voice, could understand nearly everything. What evidence, asked the magistrate, had been secured by the prosecution to prove this most interesting theory? First, there was the affidavit of Emilienne Sarell, who could only say that this man was not unlike a man she had seen in the theatre on the day of the fire. That was not very satisfactory. But chiefly they had the evidence of the pharmacist Lizarda. He had undoubtedly sold an ounce of permanganate of potash to the prisoner: the prisoner admitted it. He required it for disinfecting his goats, a worthy and not unnatural motive. The pharmacist Lizarda further stated that on the same day he had missed a bottle of glycerine. The connection between the two substances was interesting, but had it been proved that Garcia was a thief? By no means. It had been missed after Garcia's visit, but forty or fifty other persons had been in the shop also on that day. Lizarda had not reported the theft. Perhaps a whisper of what was required to prove a certain theory had reached him. The court had to inquire whether there was a case for the prisoner to answer, and at all events as it was now nearly twelve o'clock it would adjourn for three hours. The court would meet again in the name of the Republic of San Rocco at three o'clock.

Simmonds was eating a not very joyous meal of dried cod fried in oil with the pleasant rascal of a lawyer in a restaurant which might suit the San Roccan palate but didn't that of Simmonds, when a message was brought that her Excellency was outside and would like to have a word with him. Carlotta was sitting in the English automobile of which she was so proud, and her face fell as Simmonds described the atmosphere of the court.

'But you don't surprise me. They're biased because Garcia is a San Roccan, and you're not. There was a skit last night about Señor Zaragoza in one of the cafés—San Rocco is lamentably nationalistic—I am a San Roccan, but I am under no illusions as to the mentality of my countrymen.'

'Perhaps it's my fault,' Simmonds said humbly. 'I didn't have much time to prepare my case. Mr Wilkinson's out at Garcia's farm, searching it, now. I didn't know I should have to present the full case so soon. It took me by surprise.'

'Isn't that your custom?'

'No, ma'am. In England the accused is brought before the magistrates, but, if the police ask for it, he's simply remanded until we're ready.'

'That is extremely reasonable—' Carlotta pulled a fancy note-book from the upholstery of the car. 'I must note that, and perhaps we can alter it. Here, unluckily, a man is considered innocent until he is proved guilty.'

'If they begin to change the judicial system on account of me,' thought Simmonds as he returned to the restaurant, 'it's time I went home.' As he ate his oily dish he sighed for the land of roast beef and two vegetables. These dreams were cut short by the arrival of Aubrey, who was as excited as that young man ever deigned to be.

'Well?'

'*Very* well.' He set a long brown paper parcel on the seat beside him and called for the menu, and nothing would make him speak until they had all returned to the room in the court buildings which had been set aside for them.

'I didn't want to produce it in public,' he then said, undoing the parcel, 'but if this isn't the blunt instrument, I don't know what is.'

Aubrey's treasure was a piece of wood shaped like a club, about two feet along. The broader end was padded with rubber, and there was a small hole which might well have been the seating for the needle-like spike.

'It's perfectly clear—we'll get him on the murder charge. I found this under Garcia's bed. It fits in all round—this rubber would prevent any bruising, and if we get the needle from Falzego we can show that it fits into that hole. We have a very nice little case, don't you think?'

The lawyer thought so, at any rate: he was closeted for half an hour with the magistrates, and when the court reopened it was announced that the charge of murder had been added to the other charges. Although the minor charges had not been proved, there was sufficient evidence on the graver one for the case to go forward to trial. As the minor charges were contributory to the case, they might be re-opened before the higher court.

Simmonds almost regretted his success, but he couldn't avoid his duty. Pero was not enthusiastic:

'A long sentence for Garcia does not help me. He is evidently only a tool, and a new one will be found. Now he has passed out of your hands it is in no one's interest to extract information from him.'

'Mr Zaragoza, I acted as near the wind as I dared by arresting him. If I'd given him the works—there would have been a noise.'

'Zut! They would have understood that in this country.'

'And, anyhow, that's not in my line at all.'

But Simmonds, who was nothing if not practical, rather wished it had been. He wished so even more when the trial opened a few days later. Again he had been hurried—he suspected manœuvres on the part of someone to have Garcia's case pushed forward. Feverish work, however, had enabled him to prepare a very sound case. One thing that mystified him was the silence of Sixola—not a word had been heard from that man. That things were not to run easily was obvious when the president of the court —as in the magistrates' court there was no jury but a panel of judges—waved the prosecutor aside as he rose to open.

'Since,' he said gravely, 'it is in the power of the high court to conduct proceedings as may seem best for the swift and economical administration of justice, we do not in the first place call upon the prosecution, but upon the defence, as it seems likely, having heard the arguments of both sides as submitted by the clerk of the lower court, that the defence will bring forward certain legal points which must be decided upon before the case can proceed.'

If the murder charge had been a sensation at the previous hearing, the submission of the thin-faced lawyer for the defence was even more of a sensation now. He argued that the court had no right to try Garcia as his arrest had been illegal, that even the committal order of his Excellency had been of doubtful validity. There was here a little peroration upon liberty. It now appeared that there were many persons in the public part of the court who had deep emotions on that subject. The president hardly checked them.

'Scandalous, scandalous,' whispered the pleasant rogue, 'it is a quibble—it is not even that.'

'Can we protest?' Simmonds demanded. The lawyer shook his head:

'The president has been bribed—it would be no good.'

Bribed or not, the president of the court made a show of impartiality. The defence was asked to continue.

'But even if, learned and illustrious judges, this point is in dispute, we claim that all the evidence produced by the prosecution is suspect and inadmissible. If they bring evidence of finger-prints, we must ask what impartial party witnessed the taking of them. They produce an instrument which they say was found at the house of the accused. Who knows that they did find it there, who is a witness? But above and beyond all, learned and illustrious judges, I beg leave to recall the pharmacist, Lizarda.'

There was a stir, a nodding of heads and an assent.

'Bribed too, or scared,' murmured the pleasant rogue with a shrug, as the little pharmacist hopped across the court-room like a scared rabbit.

'Do you,' inquired the defending counsel, 'wish to change the evidence given in affidavit to the court of magistrates?'

'I do.'

'Have you decided that you made a mistake, and that no bottle of glycerine was stolen from your shop, at any time by any man?'

'I have done. No glycerine was stolen. I had only nine bottles, I never had ten.'

'Tell the court how you came to make that mistake.'

'It happened in this way. The bottles were arranged in a pyramid on the counter, with one bottle on the top. When I saw that the top bottle was apparently missing, I thought it had been stolen. But I have been speaking to my wife since then, and I find that I never had more than nine bottles. To make a pyramid one can arrange them in four rows, of four and of three and of two and of one—that is how I generally do it. But that pyramid was in three rows, of one of three and of five. That is only nine. It seems that my wife, when I was in another room dispensing a medicine, had to take down the pyramid in order to open the door of a show-case, and when she rebuilt it, she started as if there were ten bottles, and at the end there were two bottles in the top row. When I saw that, I thought that the top bottle had been removed—I had not sold it, no one had sold it. It was all a mistake.'

'That doesn't mean a thing—' Aubrey whispered furiously. 'Even if it's true, Lizarda isn't the only chemist in San Rocco. And it hasn't anything to do with the murder charge.'

The defence, however, had scored a point: with a grand confusion of issues and many outbursts of emotion they made use of it to denigrate the whole evidence against Garcia. The speech was a *tour de force*, but unnecessary. At the end, the judges, without retirement, calmly announced that they were unable to recognize the prisoner, who, it appeared, had been improperly arrested. Anyone who prevented him from leaving the court would be guilty of assault.

## CHAPTER 16

## THE MURDERER RINGS UP

Aubrey was waiting for Simmonds, who had been sent for by Carlotta. The fiasco of the trial had only amused him. In fact, he had told Simmonds, it was better for Garcia to be let free. They had to solve a mystery, to find the man who was taking vengeance upon Pero; they were detectives and not policemen. Simmonds's face, when he turned up at last, was glum.

'Of course I'm fed up,' he said in reply to Aubrey's observation, letting himself down into a chair. 'You and that woman between you—'

'What's Carlotta been up to now?'

'Oh, nothing at all. Only the reform of the whole judicial system. Juries, and the judges to be better paid so they won't take bribes, and the appointments not to be political.'

'That's all very sound.'

'Oh, yes, but she wants me to work out a scheme with her—'

'You'll end up as Lord Chief Justice, or whatever they have here. Carlotta,' he stated as a fact, 'is in love with you.'

Simmonds snorted: but could be observed later in curious reflection.

'What you need,' Aubrey said, 'is relaxation. It's pretty rotten to arrive at a dead end. But it isn't really a dead end, with Garcia at liberty. We'll keep an eye on him. But not tonight. Tonight your eye and my eye is going to be kept on the lovely chorines of the Acropolis Theatre.'

'I don't want to see any lovely chorines,' Simmonds was almost babyish.

'No, but I do,' Aubrey said kindly. 'I'm a young man and—'

'I'm not so old as all that.'

'Now I didn't say you were. I only said I was a young man, and that you were going to take me on your gold pass to make whoopee, showing, incidentally, to the natives that Captain Simmonds isn't down-hearted.'

Simmonds knew he was being petted, but there are times to be petted.

The foyer of the Acropolis Theatre was as full of notabilities as ever. Pero's business, so far from being harmed, even showed an increase. But Simmonds, whose bowler hat was by this time one of the sights of the town—and Aubrey suspected that Simmonds knew it—hurried through the crowd and lurked in Calcagno's office till the lights went down. Calcagno, who kept good whisky, commiserated with Simmonds upon the result of the trial.

'No special gala tonight?' Simmonds inquired.

'No—nothing tonight.'

'Good. I want an off night—and a gala is usually the time chosen for fireworks.'

Installed in one of the super-comfortable arm-chairs Simmonds allowed himself to be soothed by the music, the spectacle, the effect of things going on, to doze, a tired business man, too tired even to demand the traditional delights of tired business men. It was pleasantly cool in the theatre, open to the glittering stars and electrically ventilated. But then the weather of the last few days had been cooler, prelude to the wet spell which San Rocco expected at that time of the year. He was vaguely aware that the interval was drawing near, and that the Carnation was dancing the finale of the last turn of the first half. He

120

hoped Aubrey wouldn't make him get up and promenade. Aubrey was blessedly silent, absorbed by the Carnation, as everyone else in the theatre was absorbed, except, confound him, the man who was making his way along the partly empty row behind. It was one of the clerks from the office . . . could he . . . no, it wasn't a gala night. But a moment later the feared and expected happened. The clerk tapped Simmonds on the shoulder:

'If you please, sir, Señor Calcagno asks for you at once, in the office.'

'What is it?'

'I don't know, it is very important—he asks for you quickly.'

Aubrey grimaced sympathetically:

'It *is* gala night after all.'

The door of Calcagno's office opened upon Calcagno himself, who had evidently been setting his foot against it. Within Pero waited for them, his face as pale as chalk. As Calcagno turned the key, he ran to Simmonds and clutched his hand.

'A most terrible thing has happened—I have spoken to the murderer—'

'Who? What? Garcia?' Simmonds was once more Pero's tower of strength.

'No, *my* murderer!' Pero wanted his drama. 'He has just spoken to me now, on the telephone. I am going to be murdered, you must not leave me night or day—you too, Mr Wilkinson. It may be at any moment, now—here—I don't know.'

Simmonds stood as stolidly as if a bicycle accident was being reported.

'Who's going to murder you?' Aubrey inquired cheerfully.

'Ah, that! If we knew that—listen, I am so distraught—now I must try to tell you. Ten minutes ago I am in here—Calcagno is with Hoffmann down the passage. The telephone rings—always I am here at this time to study the receipts of the night—the telephone rings, a voice asks if that is I. I say certainly it is I. The voice asks how is my business. I say good, but to whom am I speaking? The voice says to a man who will avenge ruin and more than ruin. He asks if I remember the theatre called Prinkipo. Do I remember? He asks—no, I forget all he said. It was one of the Three, he complains that with all he does I am not ruined. I ask him to come to me, I will be generous, I will give him all the money he has lost. He laughs, he has lost more than money, he has lost ten years, that I cannot return. And how can he come—when Alfredo has been murdered —it is a trick of mine. I swear, no. He says my generosity is too late—"I cannot ruin your business, I can only ruin you—I am going to kill you." I pleaded, I was reasonable, I ask what I can do for recompense. "Nothing," he says, and then he hesitates. "If you were to leave San Rocco and never return . . ." But—how could I promise that—my life is here, I have a duty, to art, to the world . . .' Pero broke off, his mouth still forming phrases.

'And then?' Simmonds was not very sympathetic.

'Is not that enough? He rang off.'

'Did you trace the call?'

'Trace the call? I am told I am going to be murdered, and you ask—'

'If you trace the call, you may not be murdered.' Simmonds gestured to Aubrey. 'See what you can do. But it was probably from a public call-box anyway. Now, what sort of a voice was it?'

'I did not recognize the voice, I think it was disguised. It was Spanish spoken with an accent, but that I think was fabricated.'

'It was a man's voice, you said?'

'Yes—certainly.'

Hoffmann came forward from the background:

'You have forgotten what he said about Alfredo,' he prompted.

'Yes—he said he regretted Alfredo, it had been a mistake. He learned that Alfredo had a mother to whom he sent money. That Alfredo's mother should not suffer, he had put a thousand dollars on your table in your office to be sent to her.'

'In *my* office?'

122

Aubrey at this moment turned from the telephone:

'The last call to this theatre came from the public call-box just outside.'

'Oh, well then—' For a moment Simmonds's eye passed over Calcagno and Hoffmann. But they had been together; their voices, even disguised, would have been recognized.

The handle of the door rattled.

'Who is that?' Pero was on his toes. The Carnation answered, and Calcagno opened the door. She stared in astonishment, and then in alarm, and while Pero repeated everything Simmonds tried to fit the story into the scheme of things. He knew Pero could not have acted his state of terror: also the exchange had corroborated the existence of the call. The man who spoke was evidently the principal, the pleasure of that telephone call would not have been delegated. If Hoffmann and Calcagno were ruled out, so were Aubrey and the Carnation, for one had been sitting by him and the other had been dancing. And then he remembered that two of the unknowns had been ruled out —there only remained the Englishman, or the man with the English name. American perhaps, or even, now he came to think of it, a negro. A man might have an English name and still be far from English in appearance.

Meanwhile, Pero, having told his story to the Carnation, was arranging with Aubrey for a number of the sanitary inspectors to be enrolled as a special bodyguard.

'Until,' he added, 'the next boat for America.'

'No, no,' the Carnation grasped his arm, 'you are not going to run away.' She turned to Simmonds: 'Captain Simmonds will not fail you—you have many friends who will protect you. I will stay by you—tonight, always.'

Simmonds could not help remembering that the Carnation had a reason for not wanting to leave the island, and if Pero left he might want her to go with him.

'Well,' he roused himself, 'this won't buy baby a new frock.'

'What can we do tonight, except see that Señor Zaragoza is protected?' asked Aubrey. It was Pero himself who suggested that they should corroborate the statement of the

Voice that a thousand dollars had been left on Simmonds's desk. They left Pero, much happier now that he had got the story off his chest, and almost ready to listen to the Carnation's suggestion that it might all be a hoax. If so, it was an expensive hoax, for there on the desk lay a bundle of untraceable notes of small denomination.

'Perhaps Pero is right to be nervous,' Aubrey said reflectively. 'I shouldn't like to be murdered.'

Simmonds said:

'You're sure he is being well protected?'

'Why, yes. Two of our men have been posted in his suite, and several about the hotel. And the Carnation is keeping him company.'

The Carnation—' Simmonds started. Aubrey looked at him interrogatively. But Simmonds did not continue the sentence. Instead he tipped forward his bowler hat and moved purposefully towards the door. 'I don't think I ought to leave Pero—I'm going back.'

Aubrey took it for granted he was going too. They got in the car and drove back, Simmonds silent and Aubrey elated with the sense of action. In the lobby of the Acropolis Hotel they saw a special sanitary inspector on duty, scrutinizing everyone who passed, and even as late as it now was there were still patrons who had been for a moonlight swim or were returning from the villa of a rich San Roccan. They went up, passed down the carpeted corridors, and Simmonds opened the main door of the suite with his key. Immediately two beams of light stabbed the darkness in the little entrance hall. Simmonds might have remembered that two guards were on duty, but he had not expected darkness. His first act was to step out of the light of the torches. Unluckily, in doing so, he bumped heavily into Aubrey, and Aubrey, losing his balance, stumbled against a modern table of chromium and glass which, built for a less violent civilization, toppled over. The sheet of glass cracked with a noise like a pistol shot, and a bowl of flowers crashed into the stone hearth. A moment later two doors opened. Pero was heard calling:

'What is that?'

The next moment a revolver shot snapped out, almost cutting off his last word. It was followed by a scream of pain, more powerful than any that human throat could utter, but terribly human.

Simmonds had found the lights, and as he snapped them on he saw the two sanitary inspectors who had retreated into a corner, and Pero in his pyjamas at the door of the bedroom with the Carnation just behind him looking back into the darkened bedroom. From it came a scuffling sound and then a long sustained hiss, like an escaping jet of steam.

## CHAPTER 17

## WILD GEESE IN A STORM

Simmonds ran across the hall and into the doorway of the bedroom, pushing between Pero and the Carnation before they had moved. His hand brushed down the switch, and then he stopped. On the floor below the open window the larger of the two pumas, Saturn, was writhing in his death agony: blood poured out over his white belly. Motionless but trembling the she-puma crouched, her burning eyes turned towards the window, her upper lip drawn back. That terrible hollow-sounding hiss stopped suddenly as she turned her head and saw Simmonds. He waited for the fraction of a second: a clock somewhere began to boom midnight: the muscles under the tawny skin began to move. Then he took two steps backwards through the door and pulled it close.

At once a babble of voices broke out. To the group in the hall were added Hoffmann and Saco, in pyjamas, blinking at the light. Pero had seen past Simmonds into the room, and now he gave a sudden unhappy cry and started towards the closed door.

'Don't go in!' The Carnation was in time to seize his arm.

125

Her black hair streaked over white satin, and from her face greasy with ointment her eyes blazed excitedly. Yet it was she of them all who had control of the situation. Pero, now that the crisis was over, that the tension of the last few hours was released, sat down exhausted and lost. It was the Carnation who told Simmonds what he had not already guessed. Pero had kept the two pumas in the bedroom, as a special protection, while Aubrey's two sanitary inspectors watched outside. She for her part had gone to sleep, in spite of Pero's restlessness. She had been wakened by the crash of glass, and she had seen Pero leap out of bed and make for the door. She had been only a moment behind him. It was this which had undoubtedly saved Pero from the assassin, who must at that moment have been at the open window. But Saturn had seen him and leapt, receiving the discharge, which may have been meant for Pero, or may have been an act of self-defence against the puma.

Aubrey's voice was heard from Hoffmann's room which was at the side:

'There's a flat roof under Pero's window—but I can't see anyone—it's pitch dark.'

Simmonds, joining him, looked out. The flat roof, they could see from the light in Pero's room, ran along almost to the fire escape.

'That's how he got up. We'll go out and search the grounds.'

The clouds had covered the moon, and in a very short time they realized that search was almost hopeless: trees and shrubs reached to the edge of a precipitous hill, and then there were rocks and shrubs down a rough slope to the road below.

Simmonds ventured a few feet down the slope and then called to Aubrey to come back:

'Let your men carry on here. He must be an agile sort of a person—the same one who climbed up the other house.'

'Garcia?'

'That's what I think. He may still be hiding around here, and if he is, ten to one we shan't find him. If he's got away —where would he go?'

'Make for home?'

'That's what I think. Unless he has a place in the town where he can hide. We'll take a chance on it and make for his shack—he'll have parked the car somewhere—he'll have to get to it, and then it can only do forty. With luck we'll overtake him.'

The grey car could do a useful sixty. Within two minutes, and only ten minutes after the revolver shot, they had started. Aubrey had only paused to take a heavy spanner from the tool-kit and lay it beside him.

A couple of minutes after they had started the storm broke: rain descended as if a gigantic bath-tub had been suddenly emptied over the island. Muddy spray curved up on each side of the radiator, and the rain sluiced the windscreen beyond the capacity of the shrivelled wiper, which jerked desperately without effect. Aubrey kept his foot down, but the car had hardly reached its maximum speed when Simmonds shouted and pointed forwards. The brakes screamed, the car swayed from side to side like a boat, and if it hadn't finally spun round on its own ground like a top they would have smashed through the level-crossing gate of the railway. The car ended up with its nose touching the white bar, on which an oil lamp gleamed red. Over the noise of the rain they could now hear the clanking of wagons. A long line of empty mineral trucks jolted by; then the white bar rose slowly. There was a gleam of yellow light from the little corrugated iron cabin by the track, which was in danger of being carried away by the rushing streams of red mud and frothy water. The car bumped over the rails, and suddenly, as the forest spread before them, the rain ceased.

'It couldn't have lasted long at that rate,' Aubrey shouted. 'An hour's English rain in six minutes.

At first the car still threw up spouts of mud, but the road was mounting, and soon as they reached higher land the surface under them was a sandy beach, scattered with stones, torn banana leaves and broken branches, the débris of the storm. The moon came out and showed them the broken gate where they had to turn, and the low huddle of half-ruinous buildings. There was a light behind one curtained window. Aubrey viewed it with disfavour as he gripped the spanner and descended.

'Well, we didn't catch him up,' Simmonds observed.

'Looks as if he had been here snug all the time.' Aubrey indicated the light.

'We were held up by the rain and the crossing.'

'Two minutes, or two and a half minutes at the outside. He had twelve minutes' start—no, not so much, for he had to get to his car. Say eight minutes. The difference in our speeds, on an average, is twenty miles an hour—we ought to have just caught him up if the distance is—oh, somewhere about twenty-seven miles.' Aubrey, muttering calculations to himself, glanced at the trip indicator. He was always working out how many miles they could do to the gallon. 'Forty-four and a half kilometres,' he read. 'Well, that's just about it. We ought to have been on his heels at any rate.'

'Let's see anyway.' Simmonds led the way up the swampy drive, and Aubrey knocked on the door with the spanner. There was no sound except that of the water dripping from the broken gutter. Simmonds tried the latch.

'Bolted.'

They peered in at the window, but the curtain covered it closely.

'We'll try the back.' Simmonds started off.

'Perhaps we passed him on the way,' Aubrey suggested.

'Not unless it was right back in the town. There's no other road here, no turnings.'

'And,' Aubrey interjected, 'there's the car!'

The moonlight gleamed on the metal work of the old two-seater which stood in a broken-down shed. Simmonds stepped to it and put his hand on the radiator.

'Cold as ice.'

'Oh.' Aubrey had to feel too. 'It is. Then what do we do —creep away with our tails down?'

Simmonds was hesitating, when suddenly a voice hailed them in Spanish—a familiar voice. They swung round, to see Sixola approaching. Behind him the kitchen door was open and the light streamed out.

'Ah, it is Captain Simmonds! And Mr Wilkinson! A pleasant surprise! And you look wet—come in—come in.'

They could not ask the chief of police what he was doing in Garcia's shack, nor could they refuse the invitation. But Sixola, as Simmonds and Aubrey, who was keeping a firm grip on the spanner, followed, explained of his own accord, and the view which met their eyes when they entered the main room was explanation in itself. Garcia was sitting in an upright chair before his own hearth, bound hand and foot. A thin runnel of blood ran from the corner of his mouth. On the edge of the table perched a burly sergeant of police, a leather crop in his hand. Two other policemen, with carbines across their knees, sat on a bench.

'Perhaps you can assist—' Sixola waved towards Garcia, who glared sullenly back. 'The unfortunate legal system of this island had frustrated the course of justice. And since you seemed reluctant to employ the usual methods I was carrying out an examination on my own account. But Garcia is not loquacious.'

Garcia ran his tongue round his red-stained mouth.

'But perhaps he will be,' suggested the sergeant of police caressingly.

'And what brings you here?' Sixola inquired.

'We came—' Simmonds hesitated: Sixola as a friend and helper was even more repulsive than Sixola as an enemy. 'Well, we came to see if Garcia was here.' He explained briefly about the attack on Pero.

'And the animal is dead? That's a pity.' He looked at Garcia calculatingly. 'But we can't pin that crime on our friend—he has been here with us for a number of hours. At what time was this telephone call?'

'About ten o'clock.'

'Ah, then Garcia couldn't have put *that* through. We were beginning our talk at about that time. However, that's only tonight. We still inquire about other nights, don't we, Garcia?'

'Well—' Simmonds pulled himself together, and looked towards the door.

'Oh, but don't go. You can help, and in due time you can

ask any questions you like, and have them answered.'

Simmonds shook his head:

'No—we won't. Must get back. Wild goose chase. Lost time already.'

Simmonds wasn't as tender-hearted as all that: he thought Garcia was a murderer, and if he was suffering he deserved it. But to stay and watch Sixola—the idea made him sick. If Sixola did get any results—he would be glad enough to hear about them. They shambled out, a little ashamed of their squeamishness. Sixola from the doorway watched them drive away. The moment they were out of earshot and in a silent gear Aubrey burst out:

'What about Sixola?'

'What about him?'

'Only, did you notice his trousers were wet and muddy up to the knee. In spite of what he said, about being there since ten o'clock, he must have been out in the storm. A cloak or something over his shoulders.'

'What if he was?'

'Supposing he had been coming out from the town like us?'

'What's on your mind?'

'Nothing definite, only I haven't a good impression of Sixola. I always thought it was he who had rigged Garcia's trial—'

'But he doesn't seem a friend of Garcia's tonight.'

'That's true.'

Aubrey was silent, so silent that he was obviously turning over something in his mind. Simmonds observed that he kept looking at the dashboard clocks, and at the side of the road. Suddenly, where there was a level space by the roadside, Aubrey pulled at the brakes, reversed, and started back.

'Wait a minute, I'm calculating,' he said impatiently when Simmonds asked what he was up to. He drove the car back to within a mile of the shack, and then stopped again.

'I want to see,' he was kind enough then to explain, 'if another car was in front of us tonight. Say the storm lasted six minutes, another car, starting a few minutes after midnight, couldn't have reached the shack before it was over.'

'That car was cold.'

'I know—there may have been another hidden somewhere.'

'Yes—there'd be the one Sixola came by.'

Aubrey was out of the car, adjusting the swivelling light to fall across the road surface. 'The road has been washed as clean as a baby's face—therefore if we find any tracks, we shall know that there was a car just before us.'

'I see.' Simmonds joined him in the roadway. 'If there aren't any tracks, it means all those at the shack, Garcia and Sixola and the police, must have got there before the storm broke. And that lets them out of the business tonight.'

At that point certainly there were no other tracks except those made by their own car, going and returning—the marks clearly cut in the fresh surface.

'That settles that, then,' Aubrey admitted, bothered. 'Unless an aeroplane was used.'

'I don't suppose it was—unless it was the sort that could land on a pocket handkerchief.' Simmonds was wet and cold and disgruntled. He led the way back to the car. Aubrey drove slowly, still mutinously thinking. To Simmonds' annoyance he pulled up again when they reached the level-crossing.

'Going to look for more tracks?' Simmonds demanded as Aubrey climbed out.

'No—I wondered—we may have got that track business wrong.'

'Oh, no, we didn't. It was your idea, but it was perfectly sound and a definite alibi.'

'Nevertheless, I'm going to ask the level-crossing keeper.'

Simmonds, wet and fagged out, sat and fumed until Aubrey came back. He suppressed an 'I told you so' as Aubrey reported:

'Ours is the only car that's crossed the railway since he came on duty at nine.'

Simmonds grunted.

It was perhaps because he was still puzzling out something that Aubrey, half a mile after the level-crossing, stood on the brakes ten seconds too late: a tree, brought down by the storm, lay across the road. The car struck it with the off-side front wheel, swung round broadside, and gently heeled over. Simmonds lay on the muddy ground, and he couldn't even give vent to his feelings, for Aubrey was sitting on his head.

# CHAPTER 18

## AUBREY'S SURPRISE ARREST

In the morning Pero had recovered his courage, and though dramatized, it was real courage. The murderer had revealed his hand and the tension had been relieved. Another attack he didn't think likely—at least not yet. Only Simmonds must be quick. He grieved for the death of Saturn, and spent many hours soothing the she-puma, with such success that it ceased to be dangerous although in its nervous condition others were forbidden to approach. So far recovered was he that he went to the directors' office at the theatre as usual, Hoffmann accompanying him. Aubrey had been up early searching the fire escapes and the rocky slope. The storm had swept the hillside and washed the iron rungs. Simmonds didn't hope for any clues, but he let Aubrey play. He himself, after a thoughtful breakfast, put on his cleanest suit, and went to see Sixola. He was greeted by that gentleman with the usual politeness:

'So your car was wrecked, my dear Captain. How inconvenient. May I put my own at your disposal?'

'Thanks.' Simmonds, however, had decided to hire another.

'Was yours badly smashed?'

'Pretty bad. We left it by the roadside and came home on foot.' Simmonds was sitting in the easy-chair facing Sixola as if he was there for the rest of the morning. If Sixola broached the subject they both had in mind, so much the better. But Sixola seemed content to talk about the storm, the damage it had done to the crops, and the climate of San Rocco in general. At last, after a pause, Simmonds was constrained to ask:

'And what about Garcia?'

Sixola shook his head slowly:

'No trustworthy results. Personally, I haven't the least doubt he was directly implicated in the events you are investigating. I haven't given up hopes yet of getting him to speak, and then we shall see if your method or mine is the quicker. I hope you forgive the liberty?'

'The liberty is with Garcia, not me,' Simmonds said grimly.

'So long as you have no objections,' Sixola waved gracefully. 'I can do what would be impossible for you. What the Americans call third degree methods would not be popular here if they were carried out by yourself, a foreigner.'

'I've guessed that.'

'Ah, you realize that there is a certain amount of opposition to your work here. Public opinion moves slowly, but there is a large party here who look upon foreign institutions and foreign interference with disfavour.'

'I don't want to interfere—'

'No, no, I understand. Only you have started a criminal investigation department, which is a new thing, and now I hear you are going to be responsible for the reform of the judicial system.'

'Oh, no, I'm not.'

'But I heard—'

'It's that woman's idea. I'm not being drawn in.'

'But, don't you see, it was through you—through the trial of Garcia, that the question has been raised at all?'

Sixola was suddenly thoughtful:

'You know,' he said, 'if we could find out who bribed or threatened the witnesses and judges, presuming they were tampered with, we should find out who was protecting Garcia—in fact, the Unknown.'

'That's a thing you can do better than I,' Simmonds suggested.

'Yes. We have already narrowed down the three Unknowns to *one*—the man with the English name. It would be interesting to find out if any Englishman had lately drawn any very large sum of money from the bank.' Sixola made a note on his blotter. 'I'll see to that myself. And now—' he rose—'I'm afraid I shall have to cut this interview short. I have to meet Señor Zaragoza himself in a quarter of an hour —at a quarter to eleven to be exact.'

Simmonds wondered if Pero was giving him the air and was going to entrust things to the police after all.

'About last night?' he asked.

'I shall be interested to hear particulars—but this is a date of long standing. He promised to loan me the banqueting-room for the annual police charity gala—'

'Another gala—' Simmonds interjected with mock fear. Sixola laughed.

'Yes . . . but half the police of San Rocco will be there.' He held out his hand: 'Well—till we meet again.'

Simmonds took the hand absent-mindedly, but he did not speak the question he had been considering until he was already at the door:

'Have you known Zaragoza long?'

'Two or three years. Since he came here, but we have never been intimate. To tell the truth, I have a feeling . . .'

'What sort of a feeling?' Simmonds insisted. Sixola appeared disconcerted.

'Well, let us say it is a matter of character. That's all.'

'Now, I wonder,' thought Simmonds, as he went down the corridor, 'what he wanted me to think.' Nevertheless, he did not feel so antagonistic to Sixola as he had done. The man, after all, had good reason to be jealous.

Aubrey, hands in pockets, was walking disconsolately in the grounds of the Acropolis. He had covered the slope under Pero's window, and he had by this time reached the more level ground by the theatre. The storm had made havoc everywhere: the broken tropical flowers had already rotted to a dirty brown. Although the surface soil was already a pale lilac powder, it only had to be stirred to show that it was black and damp underneath. He was idly tracing the little deltas and creeks of sand on the gravel path outside the business entrance of the theatre block when he was bumped into from behind by someone who was hurrying.

'Now, who's fault was that?' Aubrey demanded, straightening up.

'I beg your pardon,' said the other in bad Spanish, hastening off. Only an Englishman could have mis-pronounced a common phrase so thoroughly, and Aubrey only stared after him for a moment before he recognized the English engineer —the Carnation's boyfriend—Billy Wykes. At that moment two of the sanitary inspectors appeared in the doorway— the two who were known to Aubrey as Sancho and Pilma, two of the most trusted.

'There he is!' cried one, pointing after the retreating Englishman, and they both started running.

'Hoy—' Aubrey called after them. 'What's the matter?'

Pilma turned and hesitated, the other detective-by-courtesy ran on.

'The master has been murdered,' Pilma stood to say. 'By him—by the Englishman.' He pointed excitedly to where his companion had already caught hold of Wykes's arm. By the time Aubrey came up both San Roccans were clinging to the protesting and swearing engineer.

'Gently, gently,' Aubrey commanded. 'What *are* you doing?'

'Tell them to let go of me—I've a train to catch—' the Englishman demanded in Spanish, and then added in English, 'Have you anything to do with these men?'

'I have—yes and no . . .' began Aubrey, not interfering. 'Your name's Wykes, isn't it?'

'Yes, it is. Let go, will you—' he jerked free and caught Sancho under the chin. Pilma promptly seized him round the knees and for a moment all three were sprawling on the ground.

'He's stabbed Señor Zaragoza,' Pilma yelled, raising his head from the confused mass. 'He was running away—the German ordered us to catch him.'

Aubrey decided to take notice:

'Here, I say—' he pulled at Sancho's collar. 'Let him up. What is this fantastic story?'

'Señor Zaragoza has been stabbed,' repeated Pilma, gaining his feet, but still holding on to the Englishman. 'And undoubtedly this man . . .'

'Nonsense,' Wykes broke in indignantly. 'I've just left him, he certainly wasn't stabbed then—a moment ago.'

'I think we ought to go and see what it's all about.' Aubrey appeared to be wondering what fantastic mistake might have been made. His attitude quietened the Englishman.

'Pero may have been murdered after all—it's what we've been rather expecting.'

'But I've got a train—' Wykes looked at his watch.

'You'll have to catch the next one, then.' Aubrey was pleasant but firm as he indicated the doorway. 'You've just seen him, you say?'

'Certainly, and he was very much alive then.'

'Do you mind telling me what you've been seeing him about?' Aubrey remembered that the Carnation and not Pero was more likely to be the reason for Wykes's visit to the theatre.

'If you want to know, on business connected with the railway.'

'I do want to know, rather. My name's Aubrey Wilkinson.'

'I know. You run this comic opera detective force.'

Aubrey said nothing further to ruffle the aggravated prisoner. In the doorway now appeared a knot of people talking excitedly.

'Holy mackerel,' Aubrey exclaimed, 'I believe something really has happened to Pero.'

Hoffmann, agitated for once, was pushing his way through to meet them.

'Good, good—you've stopped him.'

'They have stopped me—and I want to know—' Wykes faced Hoffmann angrily. Aubrey, slipping away through the gathering crowd, left them to argue it out. He crossed the outer office where Hoffmann had his desk and entered the big room where Pero conducted most of his business

136

and all interviews of a private nature. At one end there was a big flat-topped desk, a chair behind it, and other chairs near it. In the opposite corner, under a window through which the sun streamed, was an upright piano. Aubrey, from the doorway, could see the whole room, except the space behind the piano. A step forward revealed that there, on the carpet, lay Pero in a crumpled heap. It was possible without moving him to see that he was dead. There was a thin stiletto with a plain steel handle projecting from his back, and a circular red stain on his shirt front. Hoffmann's voice made him turn:

'Outside the door, every door, we have had men on duty. Señor Wykes was here with the master, I saw him go in myself, I was in my office. I was out for a little time, and when I came back the door of this office was open. I had some music to bring, I thought the room was empty, and I went to the piano. No one could have killed him but the English engineer, no one.'

'Hold on a minute—' Aubrey hurried to the door of the outer office and turned the key. 'Now. First: is Wykes being held?'

'Ja, ja.'

'Good. Let's take everything slowly. But before we begin—' he lifted the telephone receiver—'I'm calling Simmonds. Then we'll call Dr Falzego.'

'I have seen that man with the Carnation. Why he did this—that is clear,' Hoffmann was momentarily earnest and terrible after the German fashion.

'Hullo—' Aubrey had got through. 'This is Wilkinson. How do you do! We're having some bother here—Pero's apparently been knifed—I mean, he actually has. You'll float along in due course?'

Simmonds, at headquarters, had already rung off. Aubrey turned to the German:

'You sent those fellows to stop Wykes?'

'Ja—es is ganz klar—I saw him go in—then I was out to fetch the music—when I was coming back I saw him hastening down the corridor—I went in and everything saw, and I ran out, crying to the men.'

'All right. That'll do for the moment.' Aubrey left him abruptly and called to the two detectives who were standing in the corridor with the Englishman, who had ceased to protest. They had apparently cleared the corridor, for excited conversation could be heard from the other side of the glazed door.

'Now,' Aubrey was very businesslike, 'Wykes, you say that Zaragoza was alive when you left that room a few minutes ago?'

'Certainly.'

Aubrey turned to Hoffmann, who had followed him out:

'And you saw Mr Wykes leave—hurrying, apparently—and you went straight through to the office, and you saw no other person?'

'No person.'

'Then,' said Aubrey pleasantly, 'either Mr Wykes knifed Pero in his sleep, or you did, Hoffmann. Or else someone else did. And if it was someone else, he hid here and walked out while these fellows were chasing Mr Wykes and while you—what were you doing, Hoffmann?'

'I went to find Señor Calcagno.'

'Did you find him?'

'He was not in his office. I have sent to look.'

'I see.' Aubrey looked critically at the Englishman. He could not forget that they had been thinking of someone with an English name. On the other hand, the present murder might have nothing to do with the old vengeance motive.

'I had an appointment,' Wykes volunteered. 'The secretary will confirm that—' he indicated Hoffmann, who nodded. 'It was to talk over the sale of some land in the interior—some we wanted for the railway.'

'Quite right,' Hoffmann assented. 'Señor Zaragoza once would make a mountain resort.'

'And you were hurrying away to catch a train?' Aubrey continued.

'I said so. Back to railhead.'

Aubrey's tone suddenly sharpened:

'When did you cut yourself?'

'Cut myself—' Wykes stared blankly, and then followed the direction of Aubrey's gaze. On the underside of the sleeve of his light jacket there was a smear of red. Aubrey took the cloth between his fingers:

'Where did that blood come from—it's still wet.'

'When we were struggling . . .' began Wykes, without conviction.

'It is quite clear,' Hoffmann said phlegmatically. 'It is the blood of Señor Zaragoza.'

Aubrey and Wykes stared at the two detectives—the rough and tumble hadn't broken any skin—neither they nor Wykes had even a scratch.

'You'll have to wait a minute—' Aubrey was deadly serious. He went back into the office: there was a smear of blood on the corner of the desk, and red spots on the dark carpet between the desk and where Pero lay huddled.

Aubrey reappeared at the door:

'Wykes, Pero Zaragoza must have been bleeding *before* you left the office. As the wound must have been instantly fatal, he must have been dead before you left the office. Under the circumstances, I must exercise my powers as lieutenant of detectives, and place you under arrest for wilful murder. And if I was you, old chap, I shouldn't say a thing.'

## CHAPTER 19

### PERO'S VISITORS

Simmonds listened in worried silence to Aubrey's brief account.

'You've pretty well committed me, haven't you?' he said, upon hearing that Wykes had been detained under guard and was now in Calcagno's office. 'All the island will know about it by this time, and if we let him go we shall be charged with favouring him because he comes from the same country. The news will be flashed over the world, and it'll be in all the English papers. This is quite a different case from Garcia's.'

Aubrey's elation faded under Simmonds's cool eye, but he persisted in self-defence that the evidence against Wykes was strong.

'And if I hadn't arrested him, he'd have been away at railhead, miles away, or have escaped from the island.' Simmonds made no comment. Aubrey might be right, but the theory was too attractive for an ex-superintendent who suspected luck.

'All right, then. Let's see everything. Keep Wykes, and I'll speak to him later. I'll get the facts clear first.'

The two offices, the outer one where Hoffmann worked, and Pero's inner office, had been locked up. Hoffmann followed them in, and Simmonds did not dispute his right to be present, for there was much he had to ask him. Both rooms were handsomely decorated in a modern manner, with soft carpets, springy chairs and walls of coloured woods. In the outer office Hoffmann's desk, cupboards and filing cabinets were railed off from the rest of the room, where there were chairs for those waiting to see Pero, and a table covered with the magazines of all nations. From this office led the only door to Pero's room. Simmonds walked to the piano with his unexpectedly light tread, all his senses alert, his eyes quick to take in every detail. Standing by the piano he looked long and hard at the body of the plump little millionaire, without attempting to touch it.

'Good thing to have the weapon, anyway,' he observed. 'Funny it was left behind. Too deep in, perhaps, to draw out quickly.'

'It's a common type, unfortunately,' Aubrey informed him. 'Must be hundreds like that in the island. Half a dollar at all the shops.'

'You can try it for prints. Got your bag of tricks?'

'Yes—I was trying the sill of Pero's bedroom this morning.'

'No luck of course.'

'No.'

'Wait till Falzego's been. But don't let him touch the handle till you've dusted it.' Simmonds didn't care about leaving such important matters to Aubrey, or to anyone else, but he couldn't do everything himself, be in ten places at the same time. He looked up from the body to the window above. It was high in the wall, and the lower part of the window was not made to open. The upper panes were adjusted by a worm and cog mechanism, and at the moment they were only open a few inches.

'We can take it no one came in or left through the window—at least if it was wide open he might have come in that way and closed it up after. But he couldn't have gone out that way and then crawled back and closed it up.'

'That is just how the window has always been,' Hoffmann volunteered. 'Always so.'

'We'll accept that. Knife couldn't have been thrown through the window, either.'

'If you want to bother about the window—' Aubrey said impatiently. 'But Wykes came in by the door and went out by the door. No mystery about that.'

'Then it's a good thing to notice the window, isn't it, because that's against Wykes?' Simmonds replied.

'After seeing that blood on his sleeve—' Aubrey began.

'The blood, if it is blood, and that hasn't been proved yet, and if it is Pero's blood, doesn't necessarily make Wykes the murderer—even if he was a witness to the murder.'

'If you want to be difficult . . .' Aubrey sighed.

'I suppose you know,' Simmonds muttered, 'that the punishment for murder here is a minimum sentence of twenty years' solitary confinement. Before that time they mostly become raving lunatics.'

'You're worried because Wykes is English?'

'Of course I am. That won't make any difference to me if he's guilty. I'm only reminding you this isn't a game of charades.' As Simmonds spoke he had been following the trail of red spots across the carpet. 'Don't let anyone walk on these. Looks as if he was knifed from behind as he sat in his chair there and then staggered over to the piano. Now, why did he do that, do you think?'

'To play his own funeral march?'

Simmonds ignored that, and picked up the bundle of music lying on top of the piano.

'This the stuff you were bringing?' he demanded of Hoffmann, whose exact and circumstantial reply Simmonds was listening to as he walked back to the desk.

The smear of blood which had influenced Aubrey was along one side of the broad top, an inch or so from the edge. Its direction suggested and bore out the movement already plotted on the carpet. The top of the desk was in apparent order—blotter, stationery, letter tray, calendar. Simmonds eyes roved from that to the big safe, standing a little behind him.

'You knew all Saratoga's business?' he asked Hoffmann, who replied that everything passed through his hands. 'Then tell me, is everything in order here—anything missing?'

'Ah, I must go through everything very carefully. At the moment I can see nothing wrong. But it will take many hours . . .'

'And what about the safe? You can open that, I suppose?'

'Ja, ja.'

'Then just take a glance. You can have time if necessary for a proper search later.'

Hoffmann had hardly succeeded in opening the safe when Simmonds called him back, indicating the desk calendar which he held in his hand.

'Are these all the people he saw today? Do you know who they are?' Simmonds demanded. Hoffmann carefully closed up the safe before adjusting his spectacles and examining the calendar. It was a large one, with a page for every

142

day. Each page was divided up into quarter-hour sections:

| | | |
|---|---|---|
| 9 | 9·15 | |
| 9·15 | 9·30 | H |
| 9·30 | 9·45 | |
| 9·45 | 10 | |
| 10 | 10·15 | Penz. |
| 10·15 | 10·30 | |
| 10·30 | 10·45 | Cal. |
| 10·45 | 11 | Sixola |
| 11 | 11·15 | Vincent |
| 11·15 | 11·30 | T. & V. |
| 11·30 | 11·45 | |
| 11·45 | 12 | Wykes |
| 12 | 12·15 | |
| 12·15 | 12·30 | |
| 12·30 | 1 | |

'The big H,' Hoffmann explained, 'is for myself. I always have the first half hour or more in the morning. Then follow Señor Penzuela and Señor Calcagno. This is routine. Then Sixola was here for a little—'

'What for?' asked Simmonds, checking up on the knowledge he had.

'For the police charity gala. I made the appointment for him myself. Then there was Ramon Vincent, he is a dress designer from New York, and then Tancred and Viola, two speciality dancers. After they had gone came Mr Wykes.' Hoffmann's eye caught the body of Pero. 'And he is the last of all.'

'What do you know about these people—these dancers and dress designers?'

'I have not seen them before today. Vincent has been engaged by agent to work here. The others—I think they came to get work. I did not hear if they were successful.'

'You know where to get hold of them?'

'Yes, indeed.'

'Then you'd better do it. And what about *you*—when did you last see Saratoga?'

143

'When I was with him this morning. Not after ten o'clock certainly; I have my own work. But for all the time I was at my desk in the next office, and I saw them go in and out. When one comes out there is a bell and I wait for that before sending the next one in.'

'All right, then. Get started in rounding up those people.'

When Hoffmann had gone on that errand Aubrey looked at Simmonds:

'Hoffmann discovered the body—on his own showing he was here alone after Wykes had left. I don't think I suspect him, but if it wasn't Wykes, then it must have been Hoffmann.'

Simmonds didn't have to answer, as at that moment there was a knock on the locked door, and the voice of one of the guards announced that Dr Falzego had arrived.

'Well, it is not a needle this time,' he observed, with a not very kindly smile to Aubrey, as he stooped by the body. His examination was, to Simmonds's practised eye, convincing and professional.

'The heart has undoubtedly been pierced. The blow was not quite direct—Zaragoza must have turned at the last moment. Death was instantaneous.'

'Then he couldn't have staggered from the chair to that piano?'

'Almost impossible. It is much more likely that he was dragged or carried.'

Aubrey, who had been out to fetch his finger-print apparatus, now returned, and was told the verdict.

'It looks, then, as if there'd been an ineffectual attempt to hide the body. Can I have the stiletto now?'

Simmonds looked to the doctor, who nodded, and Aubrey set to work with the white powder and camel hair brush.

'And how long has he been dead?' Simmonds thought it worth while asking. Falzego pursed his lips.

'An hour, more or less.'

Simmonds glanced at his watch, which said half-past twelve. Hoffmann discovered the murder at twelve, roughly, and Wykes left a moment or two before. On the other hand, according to the desk calendar, he started the interview at half-past eleven. If Pero had been dead an hour it meant that Wykes must have stabbed him almost at once, hidden the body behind the piano, and then waited until the coast was clear—that moment when Hoffmann was out of the waiting-room fetching the music.

'Do you mind talking and moving about in here, you two,' Simmonds asked. 'I'm going next door to see what I can hear.'

He noticed on the way that the communicating door was of thick laminated wood, and it proved impossible from anywhere in the waiting-room, except quite close against the door, to hear if Aubrey and Falzego were obeying his request. He came back:

'Well, Hoffmann might not have heard anything.'

'If Pero's been dead an hour,' insisted Aubrey, 'Wykes *must* have been here with the dead body, even if he didn't do the actual murder.'

'I know, I know.'

Aubrey re-applied himself to the dusting, and Simmonds watched while Falzego stood by.

'Something's coming up,' Aubrey exclaimed, as a regular system of lines began to show on the handle of the stiletto.

'Gloves!' Simmonds suddenly gave the verdict, with perverse pleasure rather than disappointment. 'Cotton gloves, you can see the fabric markings. If Wykes had gloves he must have got rid of them, unless they're on him now. Better look around.'

'That proves intention—and that the murderer had time to put them on without Pero noticing.'

'You go off and look for those gloves. Search Wykes. I'm going to see if Hoffmann's collected those other visitors.'

Going out with Falzego, Simmonds arranged for the body to be taken to the mortuary at the public hospital.

'You're quite sure he's been dead an hour?' Simmonds queried.

'An hour at the least.'

In one of the dressing-rooms Hoffmann had mustered the

145

three other visitors of the morning. Before questioning them, Simmonds spoke to the two managers, who insisted that nothing out of the usual routine had passed during their morning conferences with Pero.

'Vincent' was the trade name of a German-American-Jew, a youngish middle-aged man, modishly dressed. He was very upset, naturally, that he should have come all the way from New York, by a boat which had arrived only the previous day, and that his first meeting with his new employer should be his last. Simmonds carefully went over the circumstances of that meeting: he had arrived for his appointment a few minutes before eleven o'clock, and been shown to the waiting-room, where Hoffmann had told him that Señor Zaragoza would soon be free. After a few minutes the buzzer had sounded and the secretary had indicated for him to go in. He had been greeted warmly: the conversation had been mostly general, about the New York stage and his past successes. Señor Zaragoza had been quite charming, and all the business points which he brought up had been readily granted. On leaving he had seen the two dancers waiting in the outer office, and had spoken to them: he had met them on the boat, and wished them luck, for they had been having rather a difficult time in New York. Their turn was eccentric and highbrow and they hoped much from the letter of introduction they brought from a friend of Señor Zaragoza.

Tancred and Viola also had names which were hard to spell: of central European extraction, they spoke English with difficulty. Yes, they had met Vincent on the boat, but his name was well known to them. He had promised to speak of them to Señor Zaragoza, and that preparation and the letter of introduction which they carried had stood them in good stead. They had been promised an audition for that same afternoon and the contract had been discussed in generous terms.

'Now,' asked Viola, a dark Russian type, 'what will happen here? Will the theatre continue? We have made an expensive journey, it seems, for nothing. But that is always the same with us, we are artists, we only demand the right

146

to perform, and luck is always against us.'

Simmonds formally asked them to let him know before they left the island, but it was clear that these three persons had everything to lose by the death of Pero. The Russian dancer had raised a point which Simmonds now took up with Hoffmann:

'What's going to happen to the theatre—is it a company, or what?'

Hoffmann visibly started:

'No—it was all private, all private to Señor Zaragoza. There is no company at all, everything was in his personal hands.'

'Then—' The full effect of Pero's death was borne upon Simmonds.

'Then—for whom are we working?' supplied Hoffmann. 'Who will pay me, who will pay you?'

'What about children—relatives? Is there a will?'

'He was never married—a will . . . he must have left one. I do not know anything about that. There is a lawyer in New York, and another one in the island. I will inquire.'

'Yes, get that lawyer here.' So many people to see, so much to be done, but Simmonds was taking things in his stride now. There followed a busy half-hour—had the news been broken to the Carnation? Where was she? Had the British consul been informed of Wykes's arrest? Then he had to satisfy himself that every means of access to the office block had been guarded or watched, and that no unauthorized persons had been seen. Then, at a time when he least wanted the duel of personalities, Sixola was announced.

Sixola, however, for once was quite grave and direct, almost anxious. He had seen Aubrey, and learned the details:

'It is all the more terrible for me because after our meeting this morning I was here with Señor Zaragoza discussing proposals for his safety. I had—I hope you do not mind—offered him police protection. But my offer has come too late. Everything I can do to help you, dear Captain, I will.'

'Thanks.'

'Have you examined Wykes yet?'

'Not yet—do you wish to?'

'Me? Oh, no. Sometimes I have been a little jealous of your presence in San Rocco, but let us forget that, let us work together. This man is a countryman of yours, I will not interfere. I think you have almost now solved the mystery, I will not take it from your mouth.'

Simmonds grunted:

'The mystery remains, even if Wykes did kill Pero. It's a matter of character—I can't believe that he is the man who threatened Pero on the telephone—the author of all the other things.'

Sixola hesitated, and then drew a folded letter from his pocket.

'If you lack some connection between Wykes and those other things, perhaps this which I have here will open your eyes. You remember I suggested that if we found out who bribed the judges we should find out who was behind Garcia. I have no proof of the bribery, but I have this: it is from the manager of the London and San Rocco Bank. I inquired what Englishmen had drawn out unusually large sums, and he tells me that Wykes arranged for a tranfer from his London account of two thousand pounds. His normal business there is a matter of forty or fifty dollars. The money was transferred and he withdrew it in hundred dollar notes on the 17th of this month, that is two days before the trial of Garcia.'

CHAPTER 20

MONEY IS BITTER

Billy Wykes flicked off an ash that wasn't ready to be flicked, and fidgeted nervously when Simmonds sat down, his bowler hat a little to the back of his head and his hands in his pockets. Simmonds felt certain that in half an hour's time he would know, even if final proof was lacking, whether the prisoner was guilty, and he was in no hurry to start his questions. He took stock of the man, whose nervousness might be well understood: he saw a strong, intelligent face, tanned and wrinkled, with something boyish and desperate about the eyes. The Carnation's choice of a lover did her credit.

'Well, go on,' Wykes demanded impatiently, 'what do you want to know.'

'Now, Mr Hicks,' Simmonds had his own brand of astuteness, 'you don't have to answer anything if you don't want to. I've telephoned the British consul, but he won't be back until tomorrow. If you want a lawyer you've only to ask.'

'I don't want any lawyer. I want to get this over and get back to my job.'

'Naturally, Mr Hicks.'

'Wykes.'

'I beg your pardon?'

'My name's Wykes.'

'Well, now, that's funny. I had an idea it was Hicks. Wykes, you say. Well, there's not much difference in the sound. Perhaps you've a relative, or you know somebody named Hicks, and that's how I got the idea?' Simmonds was almost plaintive. Wykes's negative sounded genuine enough.

'All right, then. Let me see, your full name is—'

'William Penrose Wykes.'

'And how old are you?'

'Thirty-five.'

'Oh, then you'd just have missed the war, I suppose.'

'No, I joined up early in '18. Air Force.'

'And afterwards?'

'Took an engineering degree, joined my present firm, and stayed with them ever since.'

'That would take you over the world a bit?'

'Yes, India, South Africa, but mostly in South America.'

'Ever worked in the Near East?'

'No, I have not worked in the Near East. I have never

been within a thousand miles of Turkey. Sorry to disappoint you.'

Simmonds laughed pleasantly:

'Ah, you saw what I was getting at. You've heard that story. What do you think of it?'

'A lot of nonsense.'

'Ah, well now, Mr Wykes, there must be something behind these little things. And here's Señor Saratoga dead—'

Wykes had to admit that 'nonsense' didn't cover it.

'I don't know,' he said. 'If it hadn't ended in this murder I'd have said it was an ex-employee or someone who had a grudge against him.'

'And knew all about that old story?'

'Not necessarily. That the same things happened may have been coincidence.'

Simmonds paused: the last answer had shown that Wykes didn't know about the telephone threat, or had been clever enough to pretend he didn't know. Of course, if he had known, it would only have meant that the Carnation had told him. It was worth remembering that he couldn't have been with the Carnation since the previous night.

'Tell me everything that happened here with Señor Saratoga today.'

'Why don't you call him Zaragoza?'

'My mistake—Zaragoza. I often get that name wrong.'

'You get a lot of things wrong.'

'Mr Wykes,' Simmonds hardened up, 'I wouldn't use that tone with me. This is a serious thing that's happened, and your part needs a bit of explaining.'

'Very well.' Wykes did not appear to be intimidated. 'All I can say is, I arrived here for my appointment—'

'About the purchase of some land for the railway?'

'Yes—you can prove that, no doubt.'

'Oh, I shall.'

'Look here, I haven't murdered Zaragoza. I never saw him before until today, and then we only talked business. Everything went off all right, and I was hurrying off to catch the one and only train of the day that goes right to the rail-head, and then those blasted San Roccan toughs set on me. Now I shall lose twenty-four hours and no one knows what sort of a muddle my people will be in.'

'We'll be able to get a car for you—if I'm satisfied with your answers,' Simmonds promised. 'I shall have to trouble you to tell me more about yourself. Where do you live generally?'

'In a tent.'

'At rail-head?'

'Yes.'

'But not all the time?'

'Since I've been in this blasted island, which is only a matter of weeks, I've scarcely been in San Rocco city twice —and today was the first time since Zaragoza returned with you from Europe. If you want to know, and I suppose you do, I've been to the Carnation's villa a few times, but mostly we've met in the country. We agreed I should never be anywhere where I might meet Zaragoza. What would be the good? If he knew what I felt about the Carnation there'd only be an explosion. I'd marry her any day, but you can't imagine that girl married to an engineer, sent hither and thither to any outlandish country, living in tents. It wouldn't have been fair of me to get her into trouble with Zaragoza. He's made her, after all.'

'So when,' Simmonds asked, 'you called on Zaragoza this morning, he knew nothing at all about you and the Carnation?'

'Not a thing.'

'And you parted on good terms?'

'Why not? We didn't settle the business, but it was going all right.'

'And what did you intend to do about the Carnation— in the end, I mean?'

Wykes shrugged his shoulders:

'Sorry to be obvious, but she was in love with me and I felt good about that. We'd met once before, and I suppose when the job was over I should have packed up, and hoped that—we might meet once again.'

It was just such hopeless and impossible situations that

151

bred murder. Only the death of Pero could untie the knot for the Carnation and her lover. Simmonds wondered suddenly if it was the Carnation who had done the untying.

'When did you last see the Carnation?'

'Ten days ago, at her villa.'

'She never suggested any way out of this tangle you were in?'

'No.' The monosyllable was uncompromising, and Wykes looked Simmonds straight in the eye.

'We were talking about this morning,' Simmonds continued without comment. 'When you left the office you say Zaragoza was quite well. Now, whom did you see on the way out—just exactly what were the circumstances?'

'Just as I told you—I shook hands with Zaragoza, and he rang the bell. But the waiting-room was empty. I hurried across it, saw the secretary coming down the passage with some music or something in his hands, then I passed the couple of toughs at the door, and outside bumped into that ass lieutenant of yours. The next moment they were after me crying murder and stop-thief.'

'How do you account for the fact that medical examination proves that Zaragoza was dead within a few minutes of your arrival?'

'I can't account for it. It must be wrong.'

'And how do you account for the blood on your jacket?'

'Account for it how you like—a cut finger, a bleeding nose. And I haven't any cotton gloves, either.'

'Ah, Mr Wilkinson has been asking about those?'

'Yes. I turned out my pockets for him, but I'm not going to be searched by anyone.'

'Well, we can leave that till you're legally represented.'

'You don't still think I did it? You can't put me in that dog-house of a San Roccan prison—that's impossible. You simply can't do that. I've got my job to get on with.'

Simmonds felt that it was now a good moment to spring a last question:

'Mr Wykes, do you care to account for the fact that you withdrew two thousand pounds in dollars from the London and San Rocco Bank on the 17th of this month?'

Simmonds had rather expected some simple explanation —perhaps a gamble on the stock market or on the exchange. He hadn't expected Wykes to look so utterly confused. His invention, if he was searching round for a reason, appeared to fail entirely, after a few stuttered words he said:

'That's a private matter.'

'I'm sorry, I must have an answer.'

'And if I refuse to give you one?'

'That will be very foolish of you. I consider that question of prime importance.'

'I don't see why.'

'Never mind, answer it.'

'I—I don't wish to answer it.'

'I'm sorry.' Simmonds made a motion towards the door.

'Wait a minute—what are you going to do?'

'I'm afraid you will have to remain in custody, Wykes. I'm not satisfied with your explanations.'

Wykes hesitated:

'And if I answered that question?'

'It depends on the answer. I couldn't make any promise. Besides, there are other things to be cleared up.'

'All right.' Wykes drew himself upright with an effort. 'I won't answer it. But I warn you, there'll be an unholy stink. What do you want to come to this island for, putting your nose into things? Look here—I'm English too—I give you my word I won't run away. Let me go.'

Simmonds was troubled enough in his mind, but this sort of appeal was wasted.

'It's because we come—from the same country—I can't show you any favours. A man has been murdered, two men, and I've got my duty to do. Believe me, I hope nothing is proved against you, but it's out of my hands, really, it's the magistrates you'll have to convince now.'

Simmonds's siesta was meditative: then he received a message from Hoffmann and arrived to find the secretary with an acute-looking Spaniard who wore an alpaca jacket and white spats.

'This is Señor Picacosta, the lawyer. He has the will, and now we wait for the beneficiaries.'

'Are there many?' Simmonds looked round the large conference room with its many chairs, to which Hoffmann had brought him.

'No, no. The Carnation, in chief.'

'Oh. Have you seen her?'

'Yes. I had to break the news. Last night, after the first attempt, she went to another suite in the hotel. She had been here all the time—when I went she was only just getting up.'

Simmonds was privately making a note to verify that, when Aubrey arrived with the two managers, and behind them the discreet Saco, who looked and behaved just as a valet should behave upon the death of his master. They all sat down forlornly at the long table, while Picacosta took his place at the end, rubbing his hands.

'We wait,' he said, 'for Señorita Smith.'

'Señorita Smith?' Simmonds looked towards Hoffmann.

'That is the Carnation—her name is Raquel Smith. She had an English father and a Mexican mother.'

'Not English,' Aubrey surprisingly qualified. 'He was an American citizen when the Carnation was born.'

'You knew that?' Simmonds looked at Aubrey reproachfully.

'Yes, of course—but we all conspire to hide the fact that the Carnation ever had to be born at all. I mean—that she exists now, at this present moment, The Carnation, that's the important thing, isn't it?'

Simmonds was wondering what else Aubrey might know and had erratically kept to himself when the Carnation herself entered. It was inevitable that she should be perfectly dressed, and in white, that her nails should be blood red and her ears clipped with pearls: that was her profession. But her manner of greeting them was subdued and grave, and her sitting down was for the purpose of being seated and not for the display of that world-famous dancer, the Carnation.

Pero's will, explained the lawyer, had been drawn up by

Pero himself and in his own language, but it was properly witnessed and so simple that there would be no legal difficulties. To his good friends Kurt Hoffmann, Pio Penzuela and Nicolas Calcagno he left five thousand American dollars: to his valet Antonio Saco the sum of a thousand dollars and all or any of his personal clothes. All the rest he left to Raquel Smith, known as the Carnation, in recognition of her incomparable talents and on condition that, firstly, she cared for his dumb friends, Sappho and Saturn, and secondly, that she caused to be erected on the highest point of the rock of the Acropolis a monument to himself by a first-class sculptor, to cost not less than fifty thousand dollars. The rest, the theatre, the hotel, his land, his stocks, his personal possessions, he left to her absolutely and without condition.

'How much they will realize,' said the lawyer with relish, 'it is too early to say. The income should be somewhere near three-quarters of a million dollars a year.'

It was inevitable that everyone should stare at the girl who had thus suddenly become a millionaire: whether she had been prepared for this or not, she sat looking straight before her, her mouth slightly parted, her hands folded in her lap.

'May I congratulate you, Señorita,' said the lawyer, warm at the mere neighbourhood of so much money.

'Yes, thank you.' The Carnation stood up, and words suddenly forced their way out: 'Pero was the best man that ever lived: he gave me everything, and I gave him nothing in return. If I could make him alive I would give every cent I have.'

Simmonds, who had been looking at her, dropped his eyes: Hoffmann had unaffectedly begun to weep. In the silence she had secured the Carnation began to walk to the door. Only Aubrey felt it necessary to correct the tension:

'She's more upset than I should be,' he murmured in Simmonds's ear, 'at coming into a million dollars.'

Calcagno and Picacosta were whispering together: the lawyer raised his voice:

'The decision rests with the Señorita. No doubt she will

155

not wish to attend to business yet, but obviously the theatre will close down for tonight. And then—'

'For tonight? It will be closed down for a month.' The Carnation had turned in the doorway upon catching Pica-costa's words. 'But please do not be anxious. You—all of you—will continue as before. The Acropolis was the lifework of Pero Zaragoza, he made it, it was his dream. I will try to continue it as he wished.' No one had any doubt but that she was fully qualified to do that, as she stood there proud and dignified. Her eyes turned towards Simmonds, and they were as cold as pebbles:

'And Mr Simmonds, you will please have my friend released at once. I need him now of all times. My protector, I call him my father, is dead. You imagine that my lover killed him, perhaps you imagine that I did?'

Simmonds did not intend to allow a scene. It was Aubrey who precipitated one:

'Well—' he began, but was not allowed to go on. The Carnation swung round towards him with blazing eyes:

'Yes, you—you arrested him. It was your fault, you fool. You know he is innocent, because you are jealous of him, because once I smiled at you, once you danced with me and —and—' she could not find words to continue.

'I hate to say it, Carnation—but you're being fantastic.' Aubrey spoke lightly, but he was no longer riding the top of the world. His poise had somehow slipped. 'I hope he is innocent, but the facts were against him. And the law's the law.'

'The law!' She directed herself again at Simmonds. 'You are so clever at changing the law, you and that meddlesome bitch who is the wife of the president. What are you going to do? Reform justice! Begin now, even a San Roccan judge would acquit him. Release him if it's only to save your own face!'

'I'm sorry. That's impossible.'

'Very well then, I—' Venom choked her words, or she thought better of what she had been about to say. She repeated in a low voice, that caressed the menace in the

156

words: 'Very well, then . . .' and after a pause, during which some scheme seemed to be incubating, closed the door softly.

'I don't blame her,' Aubrey said generously as they sat together at headquarters reviewing the events of the day. 'It *is* rather bitter to come in for a million dollars and at the same time find that your lover is marked up for a life sentence. No wonder she began not to like us.'

'I don't like myself very much at this moment,' Simmonds replied, 'and I don't like *you*.'

'Me?'

'Yes, you. All the way along if I've been involved in any trouble it's been through you. If you hadn't arrested Wykes I could have let him out on a string. We could always have got him later when we'd cleared things up.'

'I should have thought we had as much proof as one usually has.'

'Do you *want* him convicted?' Simmonds stared at Aubrey curiously.

'No, no. You aren't thinking of the Carnation's little indictment, by any chance, are you? My dear Simmonds, she probably wants to think I'm jealous of that engineer because she knows just how absolutely cold I feel about her. If I ever fall in love it will be with some excessively respectable girl in Hampshire, with prominent teeth.'

'Hampshire?'

'Leicestershire, if you like. Or possibly Notts.'

'All I can say is,' said Simmonds, avoiding the barrage of nonsense, 'there's merry hell down at the Consulate. The Counsellor has had an interview with Wykes, and they're going to produce dozens of witnesses to say that he never entered the city since the night of Pero's return—he was either at the railway encampment or at the villa. That means he couldn't have been connected with the earlier episodes—'

'Why not? We always agreed Garcia was a paid man. And he won't explain that money he drew from the bank.'

'That's true, but they'll bring up the voice on the telephone. We've ruled out Garcia, and we've ruled out the

Carnation. They'll say only the principal would have spoken that, and against our motive that he wanted to get rid of Pero so that he could have the girl, and the girl with Pero's money, they'll say that there's another person with another confessed motive that covers all the ground.'

'I think,' said Aubrey sensibly, 'that we oughtn't to begin to worry at this late hour. Let's worry in the morning.'

Simmonds rose and yawned:

'Yes, better get along. And now I come to think of it, I've got to change my quarters.'

'Change your quarters—but why?'

'The Acropolis Hotel belongs to the Carnation now. I wouldn't give her a handle.'

'Then come and stay at mine—only you mustn't mind garlic.'

Simmonds realized with a shock how little he knew about Aubrey: he had discovered him camping in the office but he hadn't the slightest idea what further domestic arrangements he had made. The young man was strangely elusive.

'Thanks, I'd better do that. Shall we go?'

Aubrey looked at his watch:

'Suppose you fetch your things from the Acropolis and come back and meet me here? I've got some notes I want to make before I forget them. I'm fertile.'

Simmonds hauled himself out of his chair and stumped down the stairs. Outside he paused a moment to take off his bowler hat and mop his brow. At that moment a large closed car slid up to the pavement and, before it could register in Simmonds's weary brain, two men jumped out: on his momentarily unprotected head descended a rubber tube loaded with lead. Red stars shot across his eyes, and the pavement came up and hit him again. The stars exploded into darkness.

# CHAPTER 21

## DIGNITY MATTERS MOST

Simmonds woke up in a bed with silk sheets—no novelty now for him who had been a guest at the Acropolis Hotel. But there was a subtle difference about this bed—the difference that marks a private bed from a hotel bed. There was sawdust in his mouth and his head refused to be comforted by three downy pillows. For a long time he didn't care what happened so long as nothing, not even swansdown, was touching the top of his head. Ages afterwards he woke again to daylight and the room began to get fixed in his brain. There was a point when he knew suddenly that it was a room in the Carnation's villa, he recognized the distinctively moulded door, and another moment when a voice behind him observed in Spanish that the Captain was awake. Simmonds lifted his head till he could see sitting opposite to the bed the man Enrique, the Carnation's chauffeur. He had a revolver in his lap. Simmonds minded more the rice-stalk cigarette he was smoking. He calculated that there was nothing to be done: one man he might have tackled, but his head ached and his belly was sick in sympathy. Nothing very heroic can be done with an aching head. Stirring in the sheets, he discovered that he was wearing his woollen underclothes. There was no sign of his jacket and trousers. He dozed again, and when for a third time he opened his eyes it was to see the Carnation looking down at him. He lay doggo: he hadn't thought yet what to do about the situation. It was still early morning, for the room was fairly cool and the sun hadn't risen yet above the forest trees which he could see through the window. But the Carnation hadn't just got up, for her face and hair and nails were as neat as ever: she smelt of the bath,

159

and was wearing a white satin robe. That only annoyed Simmonds.

'Well, how are you?' She was not going to let him sham sleep. He opened one eye, a whale in a net. 'Do you want a drink? Perhaps you'll be more interested if I tell you that there is some tea here for you. Pacho!'

The man who had spoken, the man who had been sitting behind him, now came forward with a silver tray of tea. It was the house-boy Simmonds had seen on his previous visit, a slick rogue. She took the tray, placed it on the bed, and sat beside it.

'Pacho—Enrique—you can go outside. Whew!' she exclaimed after they had gone, 'those cigarettes!' Leaning forward she tugged at the pillows. Simmonds managed not to wince. The odour of the tea was in his nostrils and when she began to pour it out he sat up, disgruntled, suspicious, but, after all . . . The Carnation smiled cheerfully—her dramatics of the day before might never have happened. Three lumps of sugar went into the cup. Simmonds took it without thanking her. It was American tea, fragrant and with cream. Still, it might be counted as tea. He drank it, and felt better.

'Now—' she brightly poured out a second cup from the little silver pot. 'I expect you wonder why you are here. At least, I think you must know. No? You are not in a very good humour? However, when we have talked things over quietly you will not feel the same. You will feel differently about Billy Wykes too, I am certain. You are too conscientious, that is your trouble. It does not really work in San Rocco. You know perfectly well that Billy didn't stab Pero, and yet you will not let him go. You do know that, don't you?'

Simmonds looked at her with his patented inscrutability. Her naked shoulder was not seductive to him.

'If he didn't,' he said at last, 'you've nothing to fear.'

Her face which had been smiling, almost coy, changed its character, seemed to grow larger, her eyes to grow larger and darker. Her lips, pressed together at first, suddenly parted:

'And supposing he did do it, you would have him kept in solitary confinement for twenty years—till he is an old man? Think what you would be like, now, if you had been shut up alone, forbidden to speak a word—no, you could sing, you could shout, you could curse and laugh, but no one would be there to listen—if you had been shut up when you were his age, what would you be like now? You would be mad, mad—a screaming lunatic, your hair would be white and your bones pith.'

Simmonds didn't point out that while there is life there is hope, and that was a thing that had been denied to Pero.

'But he didn't do it,' the Carnation said simply, 'because I did.'

She waited, with the expression of a Madonna for the result of the bombshell. But the fuse was damp.

'I happen to know where you were at the time of the murder,' Simmonds said casually. He didn't—at least, he had no proof, and he was alert for her reaction. She bit her lip. Simmonds began to smile. Once again a spasm crossed her face: this time it was possessed with anger.

'All right, all right. If you won't help me, I know what to do with you.' She rose from the bed, looking back at him with calculating eyes. 'If you were out of the way I think it would not be difficult to free Billy. And as no one knows you are here, no one will come to look. And your friend Carlotta will not be in a position to help you for very long. Perhaps you didn't know that? Well, you'll see, or rather—you won't.'

Simmonds knew that she was going to pick up the revolver which Enrique had left on the dressing-table. It would have been possible for him to have reached that spot before her. It was his woollen underclothes that kept him under the covers. He expected to be shot, but his heart was stout and his pride was not unimaginative. It was imagination which kept him there, among the absurd silk sheets, and he was acting a part just as much as the Carnation, as she levelled the revolver at him.

'Are you going to release Billy?' she demanded.

'I can't very well,' Simmonds said with equanimity.

'Well, you are going to find a way.' She came a step closer. 'I give you five seconds to change your mind.'

Simmonds thought that the five seconds might be more valuably used than in staring at the barrel of a revolver, but it took more than five seconds for his brain to begin to work.

'I count ten now,' she said when five seconds had passed. 'Then I shall kill you—unless you promise first.'

'I can't promise, if I'm not convinced, can I?' said Simmonds, helping her to a way out of the absurd situation. But she wasn't ready to take it.

'Then I'll convince you!' Her lips tightened, there was a smoky streak at the mouth of the revolver and a shattering explosion. His ear-drums sang.

'I'll convince you,' she repeated wildly, and fired again. She raised the revolver a third time, taking steadier aim. Simmonds hadn't time to flinch, no time to feel any particular emotion. The third bullet was as low as the others had been high: the thin boss of metal in the centre of the bar at the end of the bed split into several pieces. After the explosion came the tinkle of glass: one piece of metal had struck the window. The Carnation was working the trigger furiously. The ejected cartridges lay on the carpet. Suddenly she threw the pistol into a chair, and looked at him, at first with the beginnings of a smile, and then with a quiver of her lip.

'I'm not going to arrest you for shooting at me,' Simmonds said equably, 'but I'm glad you missed.' The Carnation made no remark, but, as if an idea had entered her head, turned suddenly and left the room. Simmonds had a fleeting glimpse of two very interested faces, and then she closed the door with a command to her two servants to stay where they were. Simmonds got out of bed, picked up the revolver, ejected the three unspent bullets and threw them out of the broken window. The Carnation's steps reapproached. On entering she found Simmonds, draped in the bedspread, climbing back into bed. Her laughter upset him more than the shooting. In her hand she carried a roll of thousand dollar bank-notes.

'How much do you want,' she asked, 'for going away from San Rocco?'

'That won't work with me,' Simmonds said stiffly.

'Take it!' She thrust out the whole bundle: there must have been seventy or eighty notes. 'If you don't—it will go in bribes. With that, any doors will be opened. Take it, and go on your holiday.'

It was a bit tough to be offered a fortune for doing just what he wanted to do, but he continued to shake his head. The Carnation, beaten, came nearer to winning him over than by her other methods. He felt sorry for her, now that she had failed, and because he began to see how much she was in love. He forgot for a moment his rude rough measure —that if she had been 'properly' in love she would have left Pero and followed her man.

'Take it, then,' she said wistfully, 'not as a bribe, but as a payment, in order that you may work for me, to find out the real murderer. Spend it for that.'

'I'll do everything I can, in any case. Don't worry—I'll do my best. I mean,' he added cautiously, 'I'm going after the truth, that's all.'

She sat down in the chair with a little sigh.

'Have you ever been in the prison in San Rocco?' she asked suddenly.

'Not really inside.'

'I have. I was shown over once. It is just like prisons used to be a hundred years ago. There are not many prisoners in the cells because they are mostly in the prison hospital. And they live there till they die, and then they carry them out, two or three a day in the hot weather.'

Simmonds was silent.

'I don't think Billy would live very long, in that place.'

'I don't think that will happen,' Simmonds said comfortingly. 'He will have good friends to look after him—if he's ill a doctor can be sent in.'

'Then it's too late.'

'Then we'll build a new prison.' His attempt at jocularity made the Carnation break down. Simmonds cared least for his profession of man-catching at that moment.

# CHAPTER 22

## THE GOLD DISC

Aubrey had waited for Simmonds at headquarters for an hour and a half, and then he had telephoned to the Acropolis Hotel and to the little hotel by the docks where he himself was staying. No Simmonds. Thinking that Simmonds was merely stealing a march on him and not wanting anyway to raise the general alarm, Aubrey had gone to bed. In the morning, with no Simmonds, he had begun to be anxious: telephones had rung again, but just at the moment when it really seemed as if something ought to be done, a cream limousine slipped up to the Ministry of Sanitation, and Simmonds descended. He was curiously reticent as to how he had come by the bump on his head, but he had to tell something of the story of his abduction. He didn't relish Aubrey's laughter.

'I don't see that it's funny.'

'Funny! It would make a stuffed bird laugh.'

Simmonds decided in self-defence to accept the joke:

'Funnier still if I'd found myself committed to a programme of prison reform.'

'Prison reform?' Aubrey's imagination was tireless. 'We'll have to tackle that later, no doubt. I'll draw up a sketch.'

'Oh, no you won't.'

'Perhaps you're right, there is something to be said for the old variety. They may put you in a cell with a stink, but there isn't that atmosphere of a rather inferior preparatory school which is the deadening thing about our system.'

'You know a lot about it.'

'I've got imagination. I wish,' he added, perhaps in connection with his last answer, 'that the Carnation would kidnap *me*. I very much doubt if *I* should have been so

164

stand-offish, if she was indicating that I might be stand-onnish. However!'

'However!' Simmonds echoed, thinking of what next he was going to do towards unravelling the mystery.

'However,' Aubrey continued, 'I suppose actually we know now that the Carnation does suspect Wykes. If she does, then she probably didn't do it. Probably she didn't know about it. She really seemed sincere about Pero. I imagine that Wykes was mad with her because she wouldn't leave Pero. I don't think the money—the will—was considered. What do you think?'

'What?' Simmonds came out of a brown study. 'What do I think? I don't think we know enough yet to begin to think.'

'Let's find out some more then.'

'We're going to. Has the car been mended yet?'

'As a matter of fact, it hasn't. It's still by the roadside. There's been some bother about the insurance, and two repairers are going to have a little private lawsuit over the right to fix it.'

'We'll have to pick up something then,' Simmonds said, leading the way to the street.

'Where are we going?' Aubrey inquired.

'Scene of the crime. There's something about that office I don't quite understand.'

They walked down the narrow street and into a little square, where the best they could do for themselves was an ancient victoria. Its progress was extravagantly slow, even for a San Roccan horse in a straw sun-bonnet—a horse that should have been superannuated and was as disgruntled as Simmonds at finding itself still at work.

'The crowd seems to be madding a little, however,' Aubrey said in extenuation. 'Troops, or something.'

The victoria had finally come to a stop. Standing up, Aubrey reported that on the other side of the traffic block a company of the president's bodyguard was passing.

'With gun-carriage. About fifty men, and they've all got each other's uniforms on. Last year they had six gun-carriages, unless they led the same one round and round the block.'

'What is it, a procession, or what?'

'Oh, a gala of some sort, I suppose.'

'A gala?' Simmonds jumped at the word.

'It can't be the president's birthday—that was last month. It isn't yours by any chance, is it? No? Hullo, we're going on.'

The victoria finally deposited them at the foot of the hairpin bend below the Acropolis. They continued on foot, and by the time they reached the office felt that they had achieved a considerable journey. The seal on the door was intact—it was the official seal of the Ministry of Sanitation, a volcano with a Latin motto—*ex cloaco salus*. Inside, Simmonds sat down to ruminate while Aubrey flitted round busily in his usual spuriously intelligent manner. There was something wrong somewhere, that was all Simmonds knew. The Carnation's pleading hadn't shaken his conviction that Wykes was innocent. On the other hand there was the blood on his sleeve and the fact that the state of the body proved that Pero had been dead at least many minutes before Wykes left. Well now, supposing Pero had been dead before Wykes arrived? And for some reason he hadn't spread the alarm. Perhaps conscious of his motive, and frightened into doing a foolish thing. No, that wouldn't do— Pero had been alive when the dancers left, they had passed Wykes in the waiting-room, Hoffmann being there too, and the buzzer had buzzed. There hadn't been a second between the exit of the dancers and the entry of Wykes. Certainly not time for any one to jump out of the safe, knife Pero, and drag his body behind the piano. Anyway, the safe was much too small. Simmonds hauled himself to his feet and made a tour of inspection, rapping the walls. They were all solid enough. He looked at the piano. On it was the music Hoffmann had been bringing. A coincidence, perhaps, that he was bringing music? Bright sunlight splashed the floorboards behind the piano. It was hot. It would have been hotter still at the time of the murder, half an hour before noon. Aubrey had gravitated to Simmonds's elbow:

'Falzego said he had been dead an hour, didn't he?' Simmonds asked reflectively.

'Yes, but it may have been less.'

'If the body lay in the sun—no, that would act the wrong way—it would mean he was dead more than an hour, before Wykes entered. That won't do. The time's checked by too many watches, and here isn't a crevice for any one except Wykes.'

'I'm afraid you can't get round it. That's why I arrested the unfortunate fellow.'

Once more Simmonds sat down and ruminated. Then he got up, and opening the communicating door, tried various angles of vision—from Hoffmann's desk, and from the outer door.

'The war-horse sniffs blood.' Aubrey was at his elbow again.

'Blood it is.' Simmonds pointed to a smear of crimson on the painted wall, about three feet from the ground.

'It looks like blood—' Aubrey confirmed.

'Well—did that come from Wykes?'

'As he was on the way out, but—' Aubrey broke off with a whistle.

'Yes, as he was passing—but why was he passing *here?*' The smear was on the wall between the communicating door and Hoffmann's desk. To reach it one had to go behind the rail. 'Why should Wykes take that way out? Because he wanted to kiss Hoffmann goodbye?'

'But Hoffmann wasn't there—'

'No, he wasn't.'

'And Hoffmann absolutely hasn't an alibi—'

'No,' Simmonds shook his head, 'that won't account for the fact that Pero *must* have been dead when Wykes entered that room.'

'I'd rather it had been Hoffmann,' Aubrey said, disappointed. 'However.'

'Well, where was he going?' Simmonds examined the wedge-shaped stain: at the blunt end the blood was thicker. The thin end pointed in the direction of the desk. In the corner, on the way to the desk, stood a tall cupboard.

'That stain,' Simmonds had his hand on the knob of the cupboard door, 'may have been left legitimately by Hoffmann, after he had discovered the body. Or by anyone else for that matter. Or that person may have had business in this cupboard.' He pulled open the door. It was deep and without shelves. At the bottom were bundles of papers and several cardboard boxes. The boxes were crushed and the papers trampled.

'Old Mother Hubbard, she went to the cupboard—' Aubrey murmured as the full meaning of the trampled papers was borne upon him.

'Answer comes there—when?'

'After the murder.' Simmonds stooped and peered. 'It couldn't have been Hoffmann—he had no cause to hide. Someone who hadn't any business here. If it wasn't for the time of death, I should say he slipped in here in the moment after Wykes had gone and before Hoffmann entered with the music. Then he stayed here all the time you were arresting Wykes, and left when the guards had been taken away from the door to watch Wykes in Calcagno's office.'

'You'd do better with a match.' Aubrey offered him one, and Simmonds thrust it into the corners of the cupboard. A grunt heralded discovery. On the wall at the back of the cupboard, where the plaster had been left rough, there was a visible powdering of dust. About four feet six inches from the ground the dust had been rubbed away.

'Showing, I take it,' said Aubrey, 'that someone stood in the cupboard on top of the cardboard boxes and that his shoulder blades rubbed against the wall?'

'Ah.'

There was a half-metre rule on Hoffmann's desk, and Simmonds spent an abstracted five minutes, measuring and reducing metres to inches.

'The man,' he said finally, 'stood about five feet six. He couldn't crouch, because the cupboard is too narrow. Allowing seven inches for the crushed boxes and saying that there's sixteen inches between his shoulder blades and the top of his head—then that's his height. Wykes is six feet— a good six feet.'

'We never thought Wykes did stand in the cupboard.'

Simmonds didn't answer. With tender hands he was lifting out the crushed boxes and other litter.

'Clean shoes. We might find some interesting dusts, but that's too technical for this outfit to handle. And don't you—' He broke off, and, as Aubrey craned forward, dived in among the scattered rubbish and drew out a gold disc, the size of a sovereign, chased with Pero's PZ.

'A gold pass! That narrows it down, provided,' he added cautiously, 'it belongs to the man who stood in the cupboard.'

'The suggestion is irresistible.'

'A good detective resists irresistible suggestions.' Simmonds was common-sensical. 'But it's worth working on. I don't suppose . . . no . . .' He put his fingers into his waistcoat pocket and pulled out his own gold pass. 'Do you know who else had one?'

'Hoffmann might know. Personally I never qualified for one. The President had one, so did one or two other government officials, and—the Carnation.'

'Did Wykes?'

'I don't know.'

'Well, of course he didn't. Pero didn't know him. Unless the Carnation ever lent him hers.' Simmonds picked up the telephone. 'No harm in asking her.'

The Carnation, having failed in every other way, had accepted with apparently enthusiastic gratitude Simmonds's promise to leave no stone unturned. She answered with alacrity when she heard his voice. He said, cunningly:

'I've lost my gold pass. It would make things easier if I had one. Could I borrow yours?'

In her willingness to do anything she did not question how it could help him. It was enough for Simmonds to find out that she had her pass at the villa and would either bring or send it.

'So she can't have lent it to Wykes, and she can't have dropped it here herself—unless she's trying to gain time by lying. What about getting that list from Hoffmann?'

Aubrey was on his way to the door when Hoffmann himself appeared, as nearly excited as that man could be. He was carrying a large sheet of surveyor's tracing paper and a folded document.

'Good—I heard you were here. I have been going through the papers—'

'Are they in order?'

'Ah, yes, but I have found something interesting. This—' he spread out the plan—'is a map of the property where Pero would make a mountain resort. The railway wanted to come over this corner, and that part which is shaded— this triangle—has been sold—Mr Wykes has bought it.'

'He said that was his business.'

'Yes, but he has bought it privately—for ten thousand dollars.'

'Then—the money wasn't used for bribing Garcia!' Simmonds exclaimed. 'But why wouldn't he tell me?'

'I don't want to seem to be hounding him—' Aubrey said apologetically, 'but one does see—I mean, if he was buying it privately to sell again to his company, that's precious nearly a criminal offence. If Pero threatened to give him away—that would give Wykes another motive, wouldn't it?'

Simmonds grudgingly admitted it, and turned the question:

'Let's know about these passes. Have you got a list, Hoffmann?'

'There is no list, but I think I can tell you. Twelve were made—you had one yourself. I have one—it is on my chain of keys . . .' he produced it. 'The Carnation had one, and Don Miguel. That is four. The Minister of the Interior, the American and English consul, Marshal Lopez, the Chief of Police and Dr Falzego.'

'He had one?'

'Yes. One time after the yellow fever rumour—he made a report for Pero that the scare was unfounded. That is ten. Two more. Oh, yes, Calcagno and Penzuela.'

'Then this one—' Simmonds opened his hand, 'belongs to one of those—or did belong.'

'It may have been stolen, of course,' Aubrey remarked.

'We could call them in, we could find out . . .' Hoffmann began, but Simmonds was not listening to either of them.

'I think . . .' he began, and then turned abruptly to

Aubrey. 'Get Wykes here—'

'Wykes? But—'

'Here. And if there's any trouble, do it through Don Miguel.'

'Release him?'

'No—not yet; on bail, chained hand and foot, I don't care. I want him here in an hour's time.'

## CHAPTER 23

## WYKES MEETS A GHOST

Whatever decision Simmonds had arrived at he kept to himself. Aubrey had the feeling that something was going to break at any moment, but he was not so foolish as to risk a curt answer by a direct question. Word must have gone out that Sixola and Simmonds were no longer enemies, for the prison governor raised no difficulties. Wykes arrived in a closed auto between two warders. Simmonds went straight to the point and asked him about the sale of the land. When Wykes admitted it, Simmonds did not seem very interested, not even when Wykes gave the reason for an act that was of doubtful honesty:

'I wanted money badly. I hoped to buy cheap and resell under cover to my company at the price they would have to pay in any case. I know it was wrong, but someone else would have done it if I hadn't.'

'Yes, yes.' Simmonds appeared not to hear. 'You say that Zaragoza was alive when you left?'

'Of course he was.'

'There was no blood on the desk?'

'I—I didn't see any.'

'There must have been. When you left, which way did you go exactly? Show me.'

Wykes did not hesitate: he approached Pero's desk, went

through the motion of shaking hands. Simmonds noticed that his sleeve dragged along the edge of the desk, where the drop of blood, on the dark mahogany, would not have been very noticeable. Then he backed towards the door.

'"Thanks—then, I'll be hearing from you?" That's what I said. Then I closed the door—'

'All right, go on.' Simmonds followed him through, saw him hasten across the waiting-room and go out into the passage.

'At this point,' Simmonds asked, 'you saw Hoffmann coming down the passage with the music?'

'I saw Hoffmann. He may have had the music.'

'Thank you. Come back, please. You, Mr Wilkinson too.'

When they were all three seated in Pero's office at places indicated by Simmonds he looked at his watch. It was the third time he had done so in ten minutes.

'What are we waiting for?' Aubrey ventured to ask. Simmonds turned to Wykes:

'Did you ever have a gold pass?'

'No.'

'The Carnation never lent you hers?'

'Never.'

It was the first time Aubrey had ever seen Simmonds nervous: he fiddled with a button, took up a paper-clip from the desk and broke it in half. Suddenly he was alert: from outside the sound of voices, one of the Sanitary Inspectors and someone else.

'Wykes—look!' Simmonds exclaimed urgently as the door handle began to move. Aubrey's eyes too were riveted on the door and he did not see, with Simmonds, the look of intense bewilderment which came over Wykes's face as Sixola appeared in the doorway. He did see Sixola, urbane and smiling at the moment of entry, hastily control a reaction of dismay.

'Well,' Sixola looked round. 'Here I am. If I can be of any assistance . . .'

Simmonds was looking at Wykes, who had jumped to his feet.

'What is this?' Wykes demanded. 'Is it a frame-up, or

172

what? Is it a plot, because of the Carnation?'

'Whom do you think you are speaking to?' Simmonds asked quietly.

'Who? To Pero Zaragoza—the man you pretended had been murdered.'

'The poor fellow's crazy.' Sixola looked at Wykes with a whimsical frown. 'Am I a little like him? Perhaps.'

'Is this the man you talked to yesterday morning?' Simmonds pressed.

'I—I could swear it was.'

'A curious mistake.' Sixola extracted a gold-tipped cigarette. 'And now, Captain, what was it you wanted?'

There was a slight pause: Simmonds and Sixola were measuring each other: then the tension was lifted.

'Oh, yes,' Simmonds laughed. 'A small thing. I've found a gold pass, and I think it must be yours. I didn't care to trust it to a messenger.' Simmonds held it out. Sixola made the slightest of motions towards it, and then raised his hand to his cigarette.

'No, it can't be mine. I have mine. Is that all?'

'Yes.'

There was not the faintest doubt that Sixola's world had come unstuck. He knew that they all knew that the gold pass in Simmonds's hand was his. He didn't even try to cover up his exit, knowing, perhaps, that he was stronger than Simmonds.

'If that's all—' he began to move through the door, 'I have a lot to do. I should have imagined,' he added slowly, 'that since you are no longer employed by poor Zaragoza you would soon be going back to England. You look tired —may I suggest, your holiday is overdue.'

They heard him go away. Simmonds relaxed.

'That was the man you spoke to and thought was Zaragoza?' he asked almost casually.

'No doubt at all.'

'I guessed as much. Zaragoza was already dead and his body was behind the piano. That's the only possible explanation, the murder took place before you arrived, even before the time Falzego estimated, in fact not later than eleven o'clock. The body had been lying in the strong sunshine, and Falzego unconsciously brought the time of death as far forward as he could. You had never seen Zaragoza—'

'Only a snapshot at the villa—'

'Sixola is about the same build and general appearance.'

'I never suspected for a moment—'

'But when—' began Aubrey.

'During his interview with Pero,' Simmonds said promptly. 'He told me he was coming, he had a reason. He was quite open. He came in uniform—'

'With cotton gloves . . .'

'Exactly. After Sixola, came the dress designer and the two dancers. They had just arrived in San Rocco, they had never seen Pero, they spoke to Sixola too. I suspected Hoffmann, but Wykes and Hoffmann were together after his arrest. I thought it might have been one of the other visitors, but then we found the gold disc. And I remembered no one had mentioned seeing Sixola leave. What happened was this—Sixola had a perfectly genuine interview with Pero. At some point of it he knifed Pero and hid the body behind the piano. Now, if he walked out he would have to pass Hoffmann. On Pero's desk was the list of appointments. Sixola as Chief of Police would know that the others were strangers. He goes to the door and sees that Vincent is waiting. If he leaves, the murder will be discovered, and he decides to impersonate Pero until the coast is clear. He carries through with the interviews, keeping, one imagines, to generalities, or letting the others lead the conversation. The first two interviews pass off successfully. He wouldn't have been so sure about Wykes. Wykes might know Pero by sight. He might know that Wykes hadn't been in San Rocco city since Pero's return, though he only missed him by a fraction of an inch on that night. There was the chance that he had seen a photograph, and we know that he had seen a snapshot which hadn't, however, been very clear. No, Sixola wouldn't have risked it, only it was then already too late to leave. Wykes entered and settled everything by addressing Sixola as if he was talking to Pero. If he *hadn't*,

174

Sixola would have had to bluff it out in some way or another. Wykes, in saying goodbye, draws his sleeve across the desk, where the spot of blood on the dark reddish wood has been unnoticed by all of them. At last, when Wykes has gone, Sixola takes another peep at the waiting-room. It is empty. At this moment Hoffmann's footsteps are heard—he darts into the cupboard and hides there until we and all the guards are in Calcagno's office. When I asked him to come here, promising important discoveries, he couldn't very well refuse, and he never expected to be faced by Wykes whom he imagined safely shut up in prison.'

'But why—' Aubrey began.

'Now, if you ask me why he killed Pero, and just at that particular moment, that I can't tell you. I haven't even really proved that he did, but I think I've proved that Wykes didn't.'

'I suppose now,' Wykes's voice was uncertain, 'you won't go on with the charge?'

Simmonds shook his head:

'I'm satisfied. I don't know how the law stands but I'm going to take the responsibility. All right—' he saw that Wykes had glanced towards the telephone— 'tell her if you like.'

'We can't arrest Sixola, I suppose?' Aubrey asked as Simmonds tactfully beckoned him into the next room.

'We can't. Then—do we shut up shop, go home? Is it all over?'

'Not yet. Not till we've proved the case—for our own satisfaction, if you like.'

'I think you have proved it.'

'Well, I think I haven't. Are all the crimes the work of one man, and if so, are they the work of Sixola, and if so, why?'

'He had assistance—'

'It's almost incredible that anyone but the principal should have made that telephone call. And Sixola has an alibi for that.'

'Then Sixola isn't the principal!'

'There were three men in that Prinkipo business.'

'But two—no, we don't know that two of them died. We've only Sixola's word!'

'It would be a good thing,' Simmonds suggested, 'to find out if Sixola has spent all his life in San Rocco. How can we find out his history?'

This was a thing in which Aubrey could help: he knew the sub-editor of the principal San Roccan newspaper:

'And he'll have Sixola's life in the obituary file—sudden deaths aren't unusual here.'

The information they received, however, did not clear the mystery: Sixola's life for the past twenty years was fully accounted for—a steady rise from humble beginnings through minor political appointments. He had never left the island.

'There's only one thing we can do.' Simmonds had arrived at a decision. 'Talk to Garcia, and this time I shan't be so particular about the language we use.'

## CHAPTER 24

### LUGGAGE AT THE BACK

After a little delay in securing an automobile for the journey, Simmonds and Aubrey started off. In retrospect Simmonds's brilliant reconstruction, though logically true within itself, refused to knit in with the other factors of the case.

'It would be nice if it did,' Simmonds said, 'but there's no point in trying to force it. Sixola may have killed Pero for one reason, and Alfredo may have been killed by a quite different person for a quite different reason. We may be no nearer solving the mystery I came to San Rocco to solve. And this is about the last day I shall have to solve it. Sixola can't go on pretending to be helpful after this.'

'I don't see why Sixola shouldn't be removed,' Aubrey said. 'Terrific scandal, but even men in his position can be impeached or bumped off in one way or another. Carlotta would rather like the chance, I think. Then you could take his place.'

'Me? Take . . .? If you even think that way, I'll break your neck.'

Aubrey said nothing and suppressed a smile. Simmonds was still mentally snorting when he suddenly gripped Aubrey's arm and told him to pull up. It was a habit Simmonds had. Luckily there was no other traffic on the road.

They had pulled up opposite to the old wrecked tourer, which was still by the side of the road waiting for the rival insurance companies to fight their battle. Simmonds, however, was not interested in the wrecked bonnet and crumpled wings: instead, he stooped down and stared at the luggage-grid. It folded back and rested against two sockets, but at a slight touch from his finger it fell forward.

'How do you make this stay up?' he asked impatiently. Born in the age of hansoms and growlers he still seemed to resent his inability to grasp the rudiments of machinery. Aubrey showed him: each socket was provided with a thumbscrew which held the grid in place. Aubrey pushed back the grid, screwed down the screws, and made all firm and rattle-proof.

'That's all.' Simmonds was uncommunicative. 'Now we'll get on to Garcia's.'

It was the third journey they had made together to the shabby homestead. As before, Simmonds had nothing more lethal in his pockets than a pipe. The door was closed, but at a push from Simmonds it swung open. They paused, listening. Then Simmonds stepped in, barring Aubrey for a moment as he swung round covering the whole of the living-room in his glance.

'Looks empty,' Aubrey observed, following.

Simmonds kicked open the door of the kitchen, and paused again, listening. Then he stepped in and threw open the door of the only other room.

'Quite empty.' Aubrey seemed glad to hear his own voice. 'The bird has flown.' It was difficult to say how it gave that impression, of an abandonment not temporary but permanent: there were cold ashes in the hearth, and the cupboard was bare of food. Simmonds pointed to a stone trough into which water dripped from a raw lead pipe.

'Last time there was shaving tackle on that ledge there.'

'Then if he hasn't given up shaving or fallen a victim to a patent cream—he's gone.'

'He's gone all right.' Simmonds ran his fingers over the ledge, and then stooped and examined the pool of water in the trough.

'Anything interesting?'

'Huh.'

Simmonds scooped up a handful of water, let it run away, and stepping over to the window examined the palm of his hand. Then he peered into a waste bucket under the sink. An empty tin of a favourite cherry preserve was the object of interest. He let it fall back, and going out through the side door poked with a stick in an evil-smelling kitchen midden.

'If I knew what you were looking for—' Aubrey hinted mildly. Simmonds did not answer, but went back into the kitchen and raked among the ashes. He found there something that he evidently expected to find, the jagged bottom of a small bottle: adhering to the glass was a dark brittle film—with the appearance of burnt varnish.

'That'll do.' Simmonds tossed back the broken glass. 'We'll go.'

'By all means. Where?'

'Headquarters. Garcia has scampered, and we want him. Your men can comb the island, and we'll comb—the only way he can leave the island.'

'*My* men . . .' Aubrey took up the point. 'Admit they've proved not without their uses.'

'I'll admit it if they find Garcia. But you, young fellow, don't do anything without referring to me. Don't go arresting anyone.'

'If I hadn't arrested Wykes,' Aubrey sweetly pointed out, 'you wouldn't have tried to make the impossible possible, and you wouldn't have been led to Sixola.'

'All right, all right. Have it your own way.'

'You're having it yours at the moment pretty much, Mr Simmonds,' Aubrey said as he coaxed the car into firing. 'I'm sitting in the dark. Well, I don't mind doing that if you think I'm not to be trusted with the great idea. But you're being rather dramatically detective, you know.'

'It's myself I don't trust,' Simmonds replied almost humbly, and then, as if continuing the thought, asked, 'We never did use that luggage grid on the old tourer?'

'No, but . . . was that a leading remark?'

'We decided,' Simmonds began, 'that Sixola couldn't have been speaking over the telephone to Pero on the night that the puma was killed, and anyway couldn't have been the man at the window, because we found him attending to Garcia, and we established that only one car—our car— had passed along the last part of the road after the storm. That is, that no one could have been at the Acropolis at the time of the attempted murder and reached Garcia's place before us . . .'

'I'm following.'

'If Sixola did speak on the telephone, if Sixola did try to shoot Pero that night, the only way he could have done the journey was—*with* us, by *our* car!'

'The luggage grid!'

'Just so. It couldn't shake out of those thumbscrews, and we never let it down. I suggest Sixola was hiding among the bushes and heard us say we were going to Garcia's. He wanted to be there first—some of his men were there, and he didn't trust them alone. So he followed along and helped himself to our luggage grid. Then, when we arrived, he hurried round to the back while we hammered on the front door. You noticed that he had been out in the storm.'

'But the police boys—'

'Must have been there all the time. We weren't a travelling Noah's Ark.'

'Beating Garcia up?'

'It looked like it.'

'But why?'

'Perhaps he'd been going to double-cross them. If Sixola

was behind everything there's no reason why there shouldn't have been a bunch of police boys in it too.'

'And Garcia's the only one who can tell us *what* they were in?'

'Judging by what we saw, he'll be glad to.'

'If he's alive.'

'Dead men don't take their shaving tackle to the grave.'

'That's true.' Aubrey trod harder on the accelerator. 'Let's hope he's still on the island.'

'He must be. There hasn't been a boat out for three days.'

'But there's one leaving at two this afternoon,' Aubrey exclaimed. 'The *Claude Grant Cooper*, for Rio. Nasty little boat with mauve funnels, and that's an indecent colour for a boat. We'll just have time to call in at headquarters first.'

Aubrey drove brilliantly, and when they reached the Ministry of Sanitation they had over half an hour in hand. They jumped out and ran in.

'Ho! Hola!' Aubrey called, running from room to room. 'That's funny! No one here!'

'What's happened to them?' Simmonds was leaving the running round to Aubrey.

'Heaven knows. I told them—always four on duty here, if the world came to an end. They've never failed before.'

'We can't wait now. Come on to the docks.'

As they drew near the fragrant harbour with its bright marine colours and blue water they scanned the shipping anxiously for mauve funnels.

'Sure it was two o'clock?' Simmonds asked, as they stopped before the office of the harbour superintendent.

'I thought so, but don't blame me if we've missed it. By half the clocks it's only two now, and we've only lost five minutes at the most.'

The official in the gilt epaulets despaired for them as he told them that the *Claude Grant Cooper* had sailed at noon.

'There's nothing else today—except the yacht of the American banker. If it is urgent—'

Simmonds shook his head:

'We don't want to travel—'

'But, of course!' the official flicked his fingers excitedly. 'The *Claude Grant Cooper* touches at San Filipo—it will be there now. If you have a car, it is hardly an hour and a half across the island, I can wire and have it delayed.'

Simmonds accepted that, action carried its own momentum. Aubrey turned the car, and they tackled the forests and the hills and the mountains: the radiator boiled and the brakes screamed on the bare iron as they shot down the last rubbly hill into San Filipo, a little town with an ugly modern church, two big factories and a seventeenth-century water-front. The *Claude Grant Cooper* was standing out in the bay, but there was a motor-boat waiting for them and two officials eating red water-melon. An impatient American officer met them as they climbed on board:

'What the hell—'

'Police.' Simmonds flashed something that might have been a warrant card. 'Let me see your captain.'

'What's the trouble?' demanded the man as he joined them, brusque but accepting Simmonds at his face value.

'The trouble is this: we are after a man named Carlos Garcia as witness in a murder case. We believe he is on this boat.'

'No such man.'

'We don't expect he registered in that name. He is a San Roccan, short, dark, big head, and I expect he has a grey beard or moustache, and short hair, perhaps rather bald. Came on board at San Rocco.'

'Murder, hey? You'd better see the purser. We had a dozen newcomers at San Rocco, and I haven't seen them all yet.'

'What's this about a grey beard?' Aubrey asked, as the captain led them towards the purser's cabin.

'Bottle of spirit gum in the fireplace and trimmings of grey hair in the sink. Also some wisps of coarse black hair blowing round about the kitchen door.'

'He might have signed on with the crew,' Aubrey suggested when Simmonds had repeated the description to the purser.

'How long would a spirit gum beard stay on if he was

working before the mast?' Simmonds remarked abruptly.

'I think I know the man, at least, there's a Señor Blasco something after that figure,' announced the purser. 'No. 33, and I think he's in there now.'

'If it's your man,' said the captain, 'take him off and then we can get away.'

They went down a corridor of white enamel and rusty iron to the smallest single berth state-room, next to the steward's pantry. Simmonds threw open the door without ceremony. Garcia was standing there, with his hands in his pockets. Perhaps he had been waiting for them. There was a straggle of blackish grey across his upper lip, and his hair had been cut away from the forehead, but nothing could disguise the shape of his head and his stature.

'Hullo, Garcia,' Simmonds advanced circumspectly. 'The last time I saw you you were trussed up with a rope.'

'My name isn't Garcia. I don't know—'

'Don't waste time. We know all about you—'

'I have done nothing, nothing—'

'We don't want to know what you've done. You've been acquitted, haven't you?'

Aubrey, as Garcia turned so that the light fell on his face, gave an exclamation of surprise.

'Eh, what?' Simmonds turned to him.

'Only—last time Garcia's mouth and face were covered with blood. He hasn't got a scratch or a bruise!'

'That's so.' Then, as a thought flashed through his brain, Simmonds smiled: 'What was it, Garcia? Cherry jam?'


## CHAPTER 25

## HIS EXCELLENCY THE PRESIDENT


'You're a blackguard and a murderer, Garcia, but I'm going to let you get away with it—on conditions. I want to know whose money you've been taking, who you've been working

for. At least, I know that—Sixola—I know that those charades at your shack the other night were staged for my
benefit. If you still swear you don't know anything about
anything, I'll haul you off this boat and whatever the law
is in this cock-eyed country I'll deal with you myself.'

Simmonds wasn't used to speeches as long and as tough
as this: but he was rattled. He realized that he couldn't hold
Garcia, and that he only had a few minutes to get the truth
out of him.

'What do you want to know?' Garcia demanded surlily.

'We want to know why Sixola murdered Pero Zaragoza.'

'Zaragoza's been murdered?' Garcia seemed genuinely
interested to hear the news.

'He has.'

'And—you say—by the Chief of Police? That's a funny
tale.'

'Don't waste our time, Garcia, or . . .' Simmonds's neck
was a fiery red and muscular power seemed to overflow the
bounds of his clothes as he stepped towards Garcia. Garcia
retreated a little, with a sick smile. But he asked jauntily:

'And the Chief of Police has been arrested by the Captain
of Detectives?'

Simmonds didn't answer. Garcia took that as a negative.
He appeared to consider for a moment and to find the
circumstance not unfavourable to himself.

'We're waiting,' Simmonds pressed. 'Why did Sixola
murder Zaragoza, why did he order you to set fire to the
Acropolis Theatre, to murder Alfredo, to destroy that film?'

Garcia smiled slowly:

'I think you may very soon find out why.'

'What do you mean, "soon find out"?'

'Was it,' Aubrey put in, 'something to do with the past,
revenge for something?'

Garcia's lips curled in spiteful amusement:

'That is very funny! You have been on a wild-goose chase
all this time for mysterious victims of Zaragoza's past. We
did not imagine you took that seriously! Oh, undoubtedly
Zaragoza believed that—he had such an uneasy conscience.
And it is true we did those things which helped the sugges-

tion. Señor Sixola is very clever. The parallel was begun by chance, but as soon as you told him of Zaragoza's fears, he was quick to continue the sequence.'

'You've been asked a question.' Simmonds did not show his chagrin. 'Why did Sixola want to ruin Zaragoza?'

'And if I tell you, I can continue my journey?'

'Yes.'

'Not that I need fear you. I am not running away—not from *you*, at any rate. I have done what I was told and taken my money. My old friends are full of congratulations, but I believe that it is convenient for me to go and join my sister and married brother. I quite understand that I know too much.' He paused reflectively, and then seemed to make up his mind. Simmonds, after all, looked as if he meant business. 'Señor Sixola is a true San Roccan. Zaragoza is a—Greek-Jew-Spaniard-hybrid, I don't know. That explains everything. But for you, who have been too busy at your detection to detect the currents of feeling in San Rocco, I must explain further. Señor Sixola did not like the millionaire Zaragoza coming to the island and bringing many interfering Americans and—Englishmen. How many small independent islands are there now left in the world that can go along in their own way without the control of another power—by police, or by tax-gatherers, customs agents or bankers? There are few. Señor Sixola and myself, and many others all thought the same—San Rocco for the San Roccans is our creed. With Zaragoza began something that was dangerous to our freedom, he brought foreigners, his money was behind the Don Miguel government. But he would not take the hint that his presence was objectionable. We hoped to ruin him—and at one time a few mishaps to his property would have been the turning point. But he recovered, nothing we could do in a small way had any effect. It became necessary for him to be removed. And he was too convinced of the benefits he provided for San Rocco to guess even that he had enemies! It is those men exactly who are the most dangerous.'

'It's perfectly true,' Aubrey remarked, as they sat in the bows of the little motor-boat, while the *Claude Grant Cooper* swung round towards the open sea, 'Pero *was* so pleased with himself, he thought everyone else must be pleased with him. He overstayed his welcome, that was his trouble. Sixola couldn't attack Pero openly, because the President was his friend, and he couldn't attack Don Miguel, because Pero's financial support made him too strong.'

'We've only got one duty left,' Simmonds said. 'Report to the Carnation and to Don Miguel. He'll have to think out what to do with Sixola. I'd have been happier to have bagged him myself, but my part's over.'

'I hope you enjoy your holiday,' Aubrey murmured.

Wykes had been left at the theatre with the two warders from the prison, and though there was no question of holding him, a formula for his immediate release had to be thought out. Sixola couldn't be given to the public as the murderer —not yet—and with the anti-foreign feeling that Garcia had stressed they had to go carefully. But the problem, as it turned out, had been solved for them. They found no prison guards, and when the intuition of Simmonds led them to the Carnation's dressing-room they came upon the dancer and her lover, sleepy and self-satisfied with the ardours of their reunion.

'Thank you.' The Carnation held out her hand to Simmonds. 'I knew you would find out the truth.' Simmonds was about to grip that hand, token of peace, when she suddenly threw her arms round his shoulders and kissed him on either cheek.

'All's well that ends well,' Simmonds said sententiously. 'What's happened to the gaolers?'

'The gaolers . . .' Wykes recalled his attention to the world. 'Oh, they went.'

'They went, did they?'

'I told them to went,' the Carnation declared. 'You're so fussy about your red tape.'

'We're going to need red tape to get hold of Sixola, lots of it. I shan't be here—he won't bother me. But you two— you'll be in danger while he's at liberty.'

The Carnation nodded: she saw the situation clearly.

'The President is the only one. Why not speak to him at

once—on the telephone?'

'Do you think . . . Don Miguel . . .' Simmonds hesitated.

'Oh, no, he'll be mildly at sea. But he'll tell Carlotta, and she'll know what to do.'

'Very well, then.' Simmonds took up the receiver of shadowed fawn from the Carnation's dressing-table and dialled the private extension of his Excellency. A voice answered indistinctly.

'Your Excellency? This is Simmonds speaking. We need your help. We believe, in fact we have proof, that it was Sixola who murdered Zaragoza.'

Simmonds broke off: the spectators realized that something had happened, they saw the blank expression of a man who has taken a hard knock, and is slow to respond, and over the wire they could just catch the words which had caused it:

'Ah, Captain Simmonds, I was expecting this call. But you labour under a misapprehension, you are speaking to his Excellency President Sixola, late Chief of Police. The ex-President and his charming wife, you may like to know, are on their way to the harbour. They expect to sail tonight on the yacht of Elvin Harrison, the American banker. There has, my dear ex-captain of detectives, been a little revolution while you were following up your clues.'

Simmonds sat with the receiver in his hand long after a click at the other end of the line indicated that the new president had hung up. Simmonds suddenly rattled the hook:

'I'll trace that call back. But I dialled the private number —he can't have been bluffing.'

'It's tough,' Aubrey remarked, 'to find that your murderer is the Chief of Police, but it's even tougher to find he has become the head of the state.'

Simmonds pushed aside the telephone:

'Dead. That means we have been disconnected.'

Wykes stood up. 'What are we going to do now?'

Aubrey took one of the Carnation's cigarettes:

'That indeed needs thinking over.'

'It's been a bloodless kind of revolution,' Simmonds ruminated.

'They mostly are here.' Aubrey had an aggravating knowledge after the event. 'I ought to have guessed what was happening—warlike preparation at police headquarters, the soldiers this morning, the disappearance of the Sanitary Inspectors, Garcia's self-assurance. I imagine Sixola had his coup d'état fully prepared, but didn't dare launch it while Pero was alive and supplying Don Miguel with the necessary sinews. Even if Sixola had the machine-guns the revolution would tend to be more satisfactory if there was a solid block of willing deputies on his side. If Pero's streams ceased, they could much more easily be detached from Don Miguel. Sixola probably couldn't hold back any longer or his revolution would go sour on him, every hour was making a difference, and Pero was still alive, and now strongly guarded—the telephone call hadn't made him bunk. It's possible that Sixola arranged the interview with Pero in the hopes that he might change sides and desert Don Miguel. Later, Pero could be got rid of at convenience. Sixola, let's say, had to reveal too much, and when Pero refused, it was simply too dangerous to let him live even five minutes longer. Or it may have been just that the opportunity for knifing him was suddenly there, and Sixola took it. The crisis, after all, was positively sizzling. I ought to have seen it, I blame myself. I've seen three revolutions in my time. They're the substitute here for general elections—bloodless, certainly. A few people may be shot. Us, for instance.'

'Sixola dare not touch us,' Wykes declared. 'Three of us have British nationality, and the Carnation will have.'

'Oh, I didn't mean we should be stood up against a wall,' Aubrey deprecated. 'I expect we shall unfortunately be shot in the rioting—that's what the papers will say. Sixola can't afford to have us going about saying that he murdered Pero, naturally. That's quite understandable.'

'While we are sitting here—' Wykes began, but Simmonds was already on his feet.

'Which is it to be—the American yacht, or the British Consulate?'

'The yacht,' Aubrey decided. 'We don't have to go through the main streets that way.'

'Then come on!' Wykes took the Carnation by the hand, and the four of them went out into the passage and down the iron staircase. Everywhere was deserted and silent. There had been no performance the day before, but there had been cleaners and porters at work that morning. They had gone now. The offices and dressing-rooms were empty, though the ventilating fans still whirled and hummed. They did not hurry, no one would be the first to show panic. The Carnation was a little ahead, she pushed open the outer door and then checked. Outside, in a little group, stood eight of Sixola's men, the sun shone on their rifles and new-looking equipment. Simmonds strode past the Carnation, and they turned and saw him.

'Good afternoon!' He touched his bowler hat in negligent salute, and started to pass.

'No, no—' the sergeant of police thrust out his rifle. 'If you please.'

'What's this? We're in a hurry!' The Carnation was matter-of-fact but commanding. The group closed round, hemming them against the door.

'Let us pass!' She took a pace forward, but the nearest policeman made a sudden movement with his rifle, pressing it against her white frieze jacket. When she drew back with a gesture of distaste there was an oily ring under her bosom.

'We have orders,' explained the sergeant, 'that no one is to go out into the streets. His Excellency is being installed in the ballroom of the Acropolis Hotel this afternoon. He passes this way.'

'In the ballroom—but I know nothing about this. It is my property, I have a right to be there.' The Carnation was indignant.

'No, Señorita, you are mistaken. The Acropolis, by the order of his Excellency, has been devoted to the interests of the people of San Rocco.'

Aubrey whispered to Simmonds in English:

'We'll try another way—the fire escape.'

Understanding the intention if not the words, the sergeant called after them as they withdrew inside:

'All the doors are guarded, you had better stay where

you are. Arrangements are going to be made for you later.'

They shut the door and stood in a group in the passage looking at each other with dismay. From the distance, from the direction of the front of the theatre, came the sound of cheering. They started to hurry, back through the empty passages, through the pass door and across the auditorium. The roof was closed, and the dark theatre lay below them in shadow as they stumbled along the side gallery. At the top of the marble staircase there was a promenade with big windows leading to an ornamental gallery. The sound of cheering grew louder as they went out and leaned over the balustrade. Below, the zigzag road was lined with police behind whom among the palms and shrubs and rocks the mob was thronging. Presently there came into view a string of autos, in protestingly low gear and with steam hissing from their overboiling radiators as they hauled up the hill ministers and officials and deputies who had, until this morning, been the ministers, officials and deputies of Don Miguel. Then, after a squad of San Roccan storm-troopers wheeling motor-cycles, came an open car bearing the arms of the republic. There sat Sixola in state, bowing and smiling, his breast plastered with medals and decorations which twinkled in the sun. From the entrance of the theatre, under the balcony, a dozen officially beautiful girls in symbolic costumes—Freedom, San Rocco, San Filipo, Victory, the Arts, Peace, Law, the Rum Industry, Bananas and Orange Culture—ran out scattering flowers, and with bouquets, garlands, ribbons and loyal addresses. Sixola's auto stopped —it had to stop, anyway, for by this time the leading cars had reached the cul de sac at the top of the Acropolis, and were being drawn up by a sweating traffic controller into an official semi-circle.

'I dare say that's the first time,' Aubrey remarked, 'you've seen a murderer decorated with garlands.'

As if he had heard Aubrey's voice above the cheering Sixola looked up. There was a flicker of triumphant amusement in his eyes, and then as they seemed to focus on something above them, the amusement died. Simmonds looked up too and at that moment from the flat roof above them leapt a tawny shadow.

'Sappho!' exclaimed the Carnation.

'The puma!'

With its tail a stream-lined rudder, an exquisite curve of taut muscle, the puma sprang. The smile on Sixola's face had hardly faded when the fangs clicked, meeting through his windpipe. Man and beast together whirled in the carriage. Sappho had avenged her murdered mate and at the same time her murdered master.

Simmonds and Aubrey were waiting among a group of reporters, consuls, officials and camera-men in the saloon of the yacht *Halico*. The doyen of the Chamber of Deputies and the members of the cabinet had been ushered half an hour ago into the principal state-room. Presently there was a stir among those nearest to the door, and the leader of the deputation appeared beaming:

'His Excellency Don Miguel has consented to resume the presidency of the Republic of San Rocco. There will be no ministerial changes and—'

'His Excellency does nothing of the sort!' Carlotta smiling but decisive, appeared in the open doorway. 'His Excellency does not resume the presidency, he continues it. We do not recognize the revolution!'

Carlotta stood aside and Don Miguel showed himself, blank, diffident and dreamy. Carlotta gave him a little push. Cameras and flashlights snapped, and the press men broke forward with a volley of questions.

'Escaping? Oh, no, my wife and I were visiting our old friend Senator Harrison. We understand that there has been a revolution, but it appears that no harm has been done. Thank you, gentlemen.' He started to amble off, but a smile of unaffected pleasure lit up his features as he caught sight of Aubrey and Simmonds.

'My dear friend, how I have to thank you! And you, Mr Wilkinson!'

'Not us, really,' Aubrey said, 'thank Saco—'

'Saco?'

'Pero's valet. He had charge of the puma, but he forgot about it and left in a hurry as soon as he heard that Sixola was holding a revolution.'

'And the poor animal was shot—that is indeed a misfortune.' He was about to pass on when Carlotta whispered something in his ear.

'Ah, yes,' he secured Simmonds's hand again. 'I—my wife and I—hope that you will accept a little token of our appreciation, and of the appreciation of San Rocco for the reforms you have been instrumental in effecting in our various departments—police, criminal investigation, the judicial and penal systems. The office of Chief of Police is now vacant, we shall be honoured if you will accept it.'

Simmonds fidgeted with the bowler hat in his hand:

'Thank you, your Excellency, but as a matter of fact— I'm overdue for a holiday.'

'Ah!' Don Miguel scratched his head, and then, stimulated by a nudge from Carlotta, he turned to Aubrey:

'Then what about Mr Wilkinson?'

'No—no—I don't think I am a detective, really. I mean, I've done nothing, and—and—I don't care about the uniform.'

'Then—have you any plans for the near future?'

'Not plans exactly, but I expect something will turn up.'

'I think,' there was almost a twinkle in Don Miguel's eye, 'I think under the circumstances we might ressurrect the Ministry of Sanitation, and now that the reactionaries have been discredited, we might even be able to pay the salary of its new—no, it's continuing minister.'